French

Quarter

Nights
& Other Stories

JR

THE LIBRARY OF HOMOSEXUAL CONGRESS
NEW ORLEANS & NEW YORK

Published in the United States of America by
The Library of Homosexual Congress
A Rebel Satori Imprint
www.rebelsatoripress.com

This is a work of fiction. Names, characters, places, and incidents are the product of the author's imagination and are used fictitiously and any resemblance to actual persons, living or dead, business establishments, events, or locales is entirely coincidental. The publisher does not have any control over and does not assume any responsibility for author or third-party websites or their content.

Cover design by Kitholeo Lai
Cover photograph by Luan Queiros
Book design by Sven Davisson

ISBN: 978-1-60864-242-7

For Terry and his enormous dick.

Contents

Introduction

The Rise and Fall of Gay Porn Magazines
by Matthew Rettenmund

In porn, as in life, everything that rises must fall.

But as usual, the ascent is so glorious, it's almost always what we remember most.

When it comes to gay print porn, the rise was particularly inexorable, from the founding of the quintessential beefcake title *Physique Pictorial* in 1951. Born of the strictly strength and health-related monthlies of the 40s like, well, *Strength and Health*, Bob Mizer's *Physique Pictorial* looked at its male subjects in a different way, or rather in two ways at once—with the sober eye of a serious, traditional bodybuilding enthusiast, and with the leer of a proud perv. Though the publication was not "out," *per se*, its mostly straight-oriented male subjects' posing straps radiated nonjudgmental availability.

This was revolutionary.

Mizer's creation spawned myriad clones, and his aesthetic—leathermen, sailors, gladiators —was also echoed in the so-called clone look of the 70s. Yet by the late 60s, the strident censorship of gay-targeted nude imagery and pornography that shaped on-the-border works like *Physique Pictorial* collapsed thanks to the courts, opening the door to publications that didn't need to masquerade as one thing in order to provide another.

Amid an avalanche of explicit porn, gay writers still longed for the biggest ask of all: a gay publication that offered sex as well as lifestyle, politics, reviews, and humor. The gay answer to *Playboy* arrived in the form of *In Touch* (1973), *Blueboy* (1974), and *Mandate* (1975), magazines that offered world-class writing, high-grade smut, fanciful illustrations and photography that could double as both jerk-off material and art.

At the peak of gay-porn publishing—in the 80s, when the gay literature boom was ramping up among mainstream and queer book publishers—these magazines and their dirty-brother publications by the dozens could achieve circulations in the hundreds of thousands, not to mention the very real pass-along potential as men shared their sometimes furtively purchased favorites with friends and tricks. They were churned out in New York, L.A., and Florida, and after *Mandate*, could be purchased not just in gay bookstores and porn dens, but right on the newsstand. In the same way *Physique Pictorial*, *Adonis*, *Vim*, and *Grecian Guild Pictorial* were boldly available in drugstores alongside *Ladies' Home Journal* in the 50s in spite of the skin they flaunted, *In Touch*, *Blueboy*, and *Mandate* were everywhere but the most conservative accounts in spite of their graphic, if never hardcore, innards.

How did the men (and women) who worked on these magazines manage before computers and in the years immediately after Stonewall? It took creativity, frugality, and the gay grapevine in order to recruit creators willing to chip in stories for low payments. It took professionals skilled at typesetting and artists able to literally cut and paste magazines onto boards. It took vision, and it took a desire to work in a gay realm and to create gay content.

Once the magazines found their way into small towns, willing writers would send their work from far and wide—and so would wannabe models. Once models were deemed to have at least two of three things (great dick, great body, great face), they would be matched to aspiring photographers, who also often hit up their tricks with the promise of appearing nude in a national magazine, something that paid very little but that offered invaluable gay street cred, proof a guy was worthy of being photographed and admired.

The pressing need to fill more than eighty-four pages every month led to innovative work, content that uniquely reflected the times and now serves as a time capsule, and it also led to some embarrassing missteps. But it was all genuine and was all created blindly as a foundation.

In this way, the magazines were both reflecting a—for better or for worse—gay sensibility, and, excitingly for those hired to do the work, *creating* it. New titles were launched monthly for years.

In the early 90s, it seemed impossible to imagine that anything could serve as a boner killer for what had become a thriving and diverse industry, choked with magazines devoted to every possible fetish. But whenever one thinks something will surely last forever, it can usually be chalked up to a lack of imagination.

With porn, it was a one-two blow that led to the demise of print titles. Hardcore porn videos for home use had become commonplace from the early 80s on, meaning men unable to get to porn theaters to see loops could screen movies at home. So why buy a magazine filled with still photos from movies when those movies could arrive to your home for maybe fifty bucks? But while the publishing industry could absorb that innovation, once the Internet blossomed as the go-to place for anything and everything, it swallowed the for-pay porn industry and re-trained men (used to holding something three-dimensional while masturbating) to simply stare at a screen, making magazines nearly obsolete.

By the end of the first decade of the twenty-first century, all the progress that had been made in advancing gay sex, gay rights, and a gay sensibility via publishing throughout the last half of the previous century had shifted—with no work required on anyone's part—to the Internet, where old and new and even homemade porn became available, often illicitly, illegally, and for free.

And it didn't wait around for monthly cycles.

This devaluation crippled porn and print, taking with them the creativity and ingenuity that had been required to churn out so many disparate fantasies on a monthly basis.

The advent of Internet porn was a boon to the consumer, but it removed pride of ownership and also the need for anything *but* porn *in* porn. When gay print porn ended, so did the unique era in which gay men strove to define themselves as whole individuals with interests that included sex.

After about 2010, it was all about sex—and there appears to be no turning back.

The Tricky Transfer

When my company transferred me from Chicago to their office in the Cumberland County sticks, I thought my life was over. At the very least, I knew my sex life was headed for the deep freeze for the foreseeable future.

A thirty-year-old "bachelor," I was making a very good salary as a database executive for one of the country's largest insurance companies, a place where I'd been a faithful employee for five years. But even I couldn't argue with the company president's logic. All the computer operations and retrieval systems were now housed in our big barn of an office downstate. It didn't make sense for me to be doing my daily job entirely by telephone, fax, and interoffice mail. And with the recession more like a depression, I wasn't about to quit a high-salaried job for the poor wages of some temporary office position, or take a big cut in my own field.

They made it easy for me, I have to say. A three-room furnished apartment and a leased car were waiting for me when I left the city for the hinterlands. Still, the initial shock of the first day at my new office left me numb.

Picture a long, wide airplane hangar with a huge parking lot on one side and a vast tundra of a frozen field on the other. Fuck, I thought, maybe an office temp job back in civilization wouldn't have been so bad after all. But I was here. I had to go through those doors.

My boss was someone I knew from his yearly visits to the Chicago office. Dick Bigelow was a rotund, misshapen, middle-aged guy who was scary-smart. What I hadn't known was that his secretary, Dotty Davenport, looked exactly like him in drag!

"Dick will be in meetings all morning," Dotty said to me as I looked in disbelief at her *Whatever Happened to Baby Jane* outfit. "Why don't you get acquainted with the office and the other managers? You'll find everything here a lot more organized than the city office you're used to."

The bitch. She knew they had me by the balls now.

Well, at least she hadn't called me "fag." Oh, they knew all right, at least all the top managers did. Still, not everybody knew. As I walked through the big building, passing rows of clerical workers at open desks and junior managers in small cubicles, every available woman in the place noticed that there was no ring on my finger. After all, at six foot one with a solid bod, a cute face, and cautiously long hair, I was a catch. But those buxom country fillies didn't know they were chasing the wrong stallion.

As for the men, well, most of them reminded me of the backwoods boys from *Deliverance*—but without the taste for male butt and dressed in polyester suits.

My best part of that first day was visiting the warehouse. A half-dozen young guys stored our tons of paperwork and took care of our fleet of company cars. They dressed in jeans and T-shirts; two were bare chested. They were hot, dumb, and dangerous. Right away I had the feeling that a couple of them saw right through me.

So there I was, a healthy, horny, young gay guy on the moon. At least that's how I felt. Even before that first week ended, I searched my national gay bar guide for the nearest sign of life. A mere fifty miles away, I discovered, was a large town with both a gay bar and a sauna. When Friday night finally arrived, I got into my weekend clothes, jumped into my new leased car, and burned rubber!

Now the bar—that was bad. The guidebook had warned that it was "mixed," but it should have said "mixed up" or "mixed nuts." At one end of the bar there were about a dozen guys, dweeby-looking young ones and some timid older ones. At the other end of the tacky club were some weird straight couples who were probably there for the "bohemian" atmosphere. That atmosphere consisted of some real old, house music tapes, and one of those plastic, lighted dance floors.

I took a seat at the bar, halfway between both groups, and imagined what was happening in Chicago at that moment. No doubt there was hot dancing at the Bistro Club, and lots of cruising at the Bijou Theater, and tons of fun in the steam room at Man's Country. All my favorite things.

At least one thing was okay about this hayseed bar, the drinks. I had four or five to show my appreciation. Then I was ready to try my luck at the nearby sauna.

A few blocks away from the swinging bar, I climbed a rickety staircase to the upper floor of a two-story building. I rang the bell and somebody buzzed me in.

Three guys in their thirties stood in just towels by a small coffee

3

counter. A little color television flickered. One guy was about six foot five and thin as a light pole. He turned his head from this side to that like a bird, checking me out. He was running the place. The other two guys were the customers. One was hairy and had wild, long hair that made me think of an electric-shock accident. The third guy was dark-haired and kind of cute, but he was real short. Like under five feet.

Beyond these guys having snacks and watching television, I could see three rows of metal cubicles with doors and, in the back, a shower room and sauna.

"I'll take a room," I heard myself say. I figured more guys would come in later. Wrong. But still, it felt good just to strip down in my little room and to see my good, tight body in the mirror and tease my cock into a hard-on.

After a while, not hearing anything but the television in the empty place, I started stroking my dick for real as I stretched back on my little bed. I was about to jerk off and get some sleep. Then I heard footsteps on the indoor-outdoor carpeting outside my room.

Sitting up, I opened the door a crack. Right away, the little guy was there, peering in. His head was just a little higher than the doorknob. But his black eyes got all round and shiny when he saw my big, thick hard-on standing up.

Next thing I knew, he was kneeling on the floor between my legs. Big as my cock is when it's poking straight up, it must have looked like a corn silo to him. And he must have been starved for dick because he went right down on it, one hand grabbing my balls while the other ran over my chest and stomach. I gave his head a firm push down while I reached over to close the door.

At the same second that the door clicked closed, his lips seemed to lock around my shaft. He bobbed up and down with such wild suction power that my cock stiffened right away to its full, thick eight inches. Man, that was just what I needed. The crazy move to the boondocks, the scary office, and worry about my next paycheck evaporated like mist. All that mattered was the hot, hungry mouth on my stiff rod.

Once he saw how much hard dick I had to offer, the little guy was having a better time than I was. I spread my legs wider and hunched my prick deeper into his throat. He met the challenge by showing me he could take it all. His muscles protested at first, then they relaxed, gave way, and my thick cock slid past his tonsils. I grabbed his head in both hands and started fucking his mouth, hard. His moans and groans let me know he liked the rough treatment. And the way he was beating his hard little cock, I was afraid he'd come before me. But this quickie was so hot and fast that neither of us could hold out for long. I guess this champion country cocksucker knew it, too, because he was going for it, full steam ahead.

My balls tightened and that indescribable feeling started to zap through my lower abs, a jolt that lifted my ass off the edge of the bed. I let go of his head as soon as I started to shoot. My dick-loving pal stayed right with me, bobbing up and down, fast and furious, as I fired bolts of hot come into his mouth.

Just when he'd drained me dry, the lithe dark-haired guy pulled off my spent cock and stretched all the way back as he shot. His tight little body looked like one of those fountain statues as his upturned rod sent a creamy streamer through the air and onto my chest. Pretty damn hot!

It was a few minutes before I came down to earth. My diminutive ball-draining buddy wasn't much for talk. He just gave me a big smile, then slipped out the door.

Later that night, I left my room to take a shower and see if anybody new had checked in. But the only sign of life was that streetlamp-shaped guy up front. He turned his head from side to side to get a bird's-eye view of me, and I rushed back to my room for a deep sleep.

Monday morning, back at the office, I was in for two shocks. I'll tell you the bad one first:

Walking toward Dick Bigelow's office up front, I thought I saw my boss bending over a desktop. It wasn't a pretty sight. The waistline and hindquarters blocked my view of the entire desk. And you wouldn't believe the tacky, duffel-bag brown slacks he was wearing.

I started to speak up. "Good morning...."

To my shock, the gigantic figure turned and it was Dick Bigelow's lookalike secretary, Dotty Davenport, wearing a pantsuit!

"Dick's waiting out back in the computer room. He's already been here for two hours," she snipped, implying that I, too, should come into the office two hours early on a Monday morning.

But as I walked the length of the long, dismal office on my way to the computer room, I had a much better surprise. There, in the middle of those long rows of desks, filled with smiling, flirting, available young women, was a hot, sexy young man. I stopped in my tracks as he looked up.

Todd Baker was blond, twenty-five, blue eyed, and gorgeous. More to the point, he was as gay as any of his city cousins, to judge from the sex vibes I was picking up. And if he was obvious to me, my unbusinesslike interest was totally queer, I mean *clear*, to him.

"I heard we had a new computer whiz from the Chicago office," Todd said, after we introduced ourselves. "I'm glad it's you."

I looked at his country-boy complexion and imagined him naked, that smooth peachy flesh all along his six-foot frame. "And I'm happy to see such a... fresh face," I blurted.

There must have been two-dozen pairs of eyes on us, so Todd smiled, bobbed his eyebrows up and down twice, and said, "Well, I guess I'll see you later." Then he returned to the papers on his desk.

On rubbery legs, I got myself back to the computer room. But when I met Dick Bigelow and a couple of his grinning yes-men in their polyester suits, my strange morning took another spin. I was told in no uncertain terms that all of the improvements and changes I had been proposing for months, long before the transfer, were being turned down.

Great. That meant my job was now that of a glorified clerk. I looked past Dick's blimpish form to the beautiful, top-of-the-line mainframe that took up most of the air-cooled computer room. I was the only person in the company who really knew how to get the most out of it, but these hayseeds didn't care about my opinions. You could have knocked me over with a feather.

Before I left the office that day, I had another encounter with Todd. You guessed it. We ran into each other in the employee men's room. Oh, I had a key to the executive rest room, but I didn't want to use it.

Anyway, we were alone in the room, and I recognized young Todd's blond hair and long, athletic body. I hesitated.

"Hi again," he greeted me, his smile growing as he pressed the flusher, then turned toward me with his cock still in his hand. I deliberately kept my eyes level with his. "I was hoping we'd see more of each other," he said, and when his hand seemed to be moving suspiciously, I looked down. His smile wasn't the only thing that was growing!

Half-hard, his cock was enough to make my knees buckle. It had a beautiful pink head and a long, wide, creamy stalk of a shaft. I didn't drop to the tile floor, but I did freeze in my tracks. If Todd had just backed into a private stall I would have surrendered and given him the blowjob of his dreams—or mine.

Instead, Todd just smiled like the spider to the fly and waved his cock suggestively before slinging it back into his pants. There was no hiding the bulge in my own slacks.

"Tell you what," said Todd, sounding like he already owned me, "I hear you got a place just a mile up the road on Main Street. How 'bout if I stop over tomorrow after work? You know, to welcome you to the company and all."

"That would be great, Todd. Seven would be just fine," I gasped. In my mind's eye I was already on my knees, sucking that beauty of a cock, kissing his balls. And shortly after his sweet load of come, blackmail would surely follow. After all, Todd had nothing to lose but some minimum wage, entry-level job.

Every chain breaks at its weakest link. Todd had snipped my weak link like a paper party streamer. As he left the rest room, I looked at his perfectly rounded buns and shook my head.

An hour later at my apartment, I sipped a big cocktail and assessed my disastrous day. Dick Bigelow's ignorance meant I couldn't even take pride in my work; I was just there for the salary. And Todd Baker's dick meant fag-baiting trouble, I was sure of that. Oh, Todd was gay or bi, all right, but he was the kind who grows up in redneck country and gets it all twisted. The kind whose boyfriends wind up blackmailed or in jail or in a refrigerator!

I reached for the phone and dialed that lovely area code, "312," for Chicago, and then a number I knew by heart. It was the home phone number of Phil Starway, one of those executive-search guys people call "headhunters."

Two months earlier, when I'd gotten the transfer order, I'd checked with Starway. He told me he loved my background, but the economy was on the rocks. I'd have to take a pay cut to find a job in Chicago. Back then, that was unthinkable. Now it seemed like a dream. And I started daydreaming about being home in the city, seeing all my favorite friends and hangouts. But I stopped those thoughts because I had to deal with reality; I might be stuck in fucking Cumberland County for a long time.

Phil Starway got on the phone and he remembered me right away. He seemed a little annoyed that I'd come to my senses a little late, but he was a pro. "Okay," he said, and I could hear the ice of his own evening cocktail clicking, "just tell me how much you earn now and how much of a cut you can live with." I told him and he promised to get back to me soon.

Hope. The first hope I'd had in weeks. Human nature being what it is, my thoughts turned back to that consummate bad boy, Todd. I guess the question of the hour was: Could I save my career and eat him too?

The next day at work was rough, but I handled some menial problems in the computer room and kept to myself.

At closing time, I ran into Todd at the parking lot. He tossed the blond locks from his eyes, smiled his wicked grin, and said, "I'll go change into something comfortable and see you soon!" I smiled and nodded and watched him run off to his old car.

I was both nervous and excited when I got to my place and started undressing. Then I saw the blinking red light of my telephone answering machine in the darkened living room. I knew it would be the job placement guy with some news.

One sock on and one sock off, I sat down in my underwear in the unlighted room and hit the play button.

"Mr. Gallagher, good news," Starway's voice barked. "Your timing is great because Federated Insurance needs a senior database guy immediately, and they already know all about you. They agreed to match your salary. In this economy, I say grab it. They say they can't pay relocation costs, but let me negotiate with them on that. I'll be out until late, but please leave a message for me tonight."

The whole world changed, just like that. I snapped on the light, punched up his number, and confirmed. "The answer is definitely yes. Nail it down," I said. I knew his commission was all the thanks he required.

Well, maybe I *could* have my cake and eat my Twinkie too. Right on time, young Todd rang the bell, and I answered the door in just my cotton briefs.

"Well, well. It's good to see you out of your suit and tie," Todd cracked, giving my right nipple a tweak as he walked by me and dropped onto the sofa. Dressed in a sweatshirt, ripped jeans, and sneakers, he looked like a college boy. Not an innocent one, though. When he took the drink I handed him, his free hand dropped to his ample basket.

My eyes were fixed on the growing dick behind the worn denim of his jeans. Todd smiled at the hard-on showing through my briefs, but we both knew this party was about his beautiful young cock.

"You know, I really hate that dead-end job I have at the office," he said, starting his sales pitch without much tact. But when someone blond, gorgeous and twenty-five lowers his zipper, you make allowances. I saw no underwear in his open fly, just golden pubes and a thick hunk of straining cock.

"Oh, Todd?" I said, playing along, as I slipped out of my shorts. "I didn't know you were unhappy at work."

His sweatshirt came up over his head, revealing his finely chiseled torso and smooth, rosy flesh. "Well, I've only been with the company a few months," he admitted, "and I *have* taken a lot of sick days after party weekends." He kicked off his sneakers and quickly slid his worn jeans down and over his bare feet. His pink horn of hard cock bounced up. "But I do think I deserve some special consideration," he complained with a whine.

I dropped to the carpet between his beefy thighs and grabbed a handful of country-boy balls. "You certainly do!" I agreed, then dived down on the solid slab of cockmeat that swung before me.

The aroma of his wiry golden bush filled my senses as I wrapped my lips around that juicy prick and fondled his meaty pink balls. The taste and bulk of that hot, silky smooth cock made me dizzy with lust.

"Suck it harder, take it deeper," Todd demanded hoarsely, running his fingers through my hair and punching his cock up at me.

I was so horned out that I didn't dare touch my own rod. I just sucked and swallowed as much of his prize cock as I could, my throat giving way to my excitement. Finally, my stretched lips

11

surrounded the thick base of his shaft and his large balls nudged against my chin.

Losing control, Todd held my head firmly against his crotch as he suddenly stood and started fucking my throat. Practically suffocating, I clutched his thighs and hung on as he ploughed my face with his giant prick. Even though I needed air, I wanted his load even more, and I met his fuck thrusts with enough suck power to make his balls tighten up and release their cargo.

Hot come filled my throat and mouth as Todd's huge prick kept driving into my face which he held in place.

When he relaxed and loosened his grip, I was still so worked up that I kept sucking his dick until it started to soften and he fell back on the sofa.

Todd's blue eyes looked hazy and lust drunk as he licked his lips and stared at me. I stood up over him and his eyes fell on my stiff cock which was hard as a rock, red and angry.

"Todd," I cooed, running my hands along the Michelangelo lines of his hips and over his firm-as-melon buns. "Todd, I just love your great ass."

I knew my luck had really turned the moment Todd did. When he rolled onto his belly on the sofa, I dove down to place love bites all along those hard peachy mounds.

"You'll use a rubber, right?" Todd asked, looking over his shoulder.

"Sure," I answered, reaching for the rubber and K-Y I'd placed under the sofa earlier. "Don't let anybody fuck you without a rubber."

"You know," he said, remembering his hidden agenda, "if you screw me at home, you ought to help me out at work."

I got myself in position and aimed my rubbered rod for the crease of his asscheeks. "Todd, I'll do all I can," I said, and I started nudging into his pearly gates. The head of his tight butthole caressed my shaft as I slid into him, inch after inch.

I was so close to coming that I knew I had to fuck him nice and slow. So I stretched out completely on top of him and fucked him with easy, steady strokes. And in a way that was better because, from my lips kissing his neck to my legs draped over his legs, I felt like I was making love to his whole body.

Todd moaned quietly as I started pumping my hips faster, and then I was shooting, fucking him harder and faster while I wrapped my arms around him. And I kept on fucking until I felt totally drained and satisfied.

When Todd turned his head and gave me a big, sweet kiss on the lips, I knew he had won, in a way. I'd wind up telling him the truth about how I was going to quit and head back up north. And when I got resettled, I'd invite him up to visit Chicago. Maybe that would be a mistake, but that's another story.

Punk Rock Cock

Mitch didn't have a Mohawk haircut or long, unruly locks, but he was as wild as any of the other punkers at the rock club that night. His thick glasses made him look bizarre, a big silver cross earring dangled from his left ear, and his denim jacket had decals and buttons of all the right bands.

At thirty, I guess I was an old-timer in that crowd, though I suppose I fit in well enough. My long black hair and leather jacket and permanent pout made me look like an original punk rocker, which I was. I also knew the band that was playing that night. I guess I really impressed Mitch by talking to one of the musicians.

The French Fries had just finished their second set, and the crowd was breaking up. I stood at the edge of the stage and spoke with the lanky bass player, who called himself Spud, while he disconnected wires and told me about his latest girlfriend.

It seemed that for every new girlfriend, Spud had three old boyfriends, and I was one of them.

"You guys were great," a voice called from behind me.

14

Spud, who had half his hair sprayed purple, seemed surprised when he looked at the fan. But he just nodded and said, "Thanks, buddy."

I turned to meet Mitch. He was short, with a medium build and dirty-blond hair. But what you saw right away were the super thick eyeglasses that made his green eyes seem kind of large and strange. I didn't let that fool me, though. I could see that he was nineteen or twenty and—behind those thick glasses—real cute.

Spud put his bass guitar in its case and went backstage, leaving me with Mitch, who latched onto me and started talking nonstop.

"Do you know the French Fries? Do you play? Do you live around here? I'm from Ohio, and I'm in town for the weekend with my father. But I got bored with the hotel and figured I'd check out this club."

All the time he was talking, I tried to look him in the eyes, but it made me teary to see his orbs all magnified by those thick glasses of his. Behind those Coke-bottle lenses, though, he was just another punk rocker, out for fun and too wired to go home—or back to his hotel.

Finally I made a decision. I told Mitch I lived right across the street and invited him over to listen to some music and have a beer. He said yes right away. On the way out the door, I saw Spud standing at the bar; he gave me a funny look like I was crazy. Well, I wasn't so crazy. I had a feeling about Mitch.

When we got up to my apartment, he tossed off his jacket and sat down on the carpet near the speakers of my stereo. I liked the way his body looked under his black T-shirt and jeans, and I started noticing the basket he was showing. It wasn't gigantic, but on such a smooth, compact young man, it looked pretty good.

Still, I was losing my nerve. I figured this innocent from Ohio didn't have a clue about what was on my mind. I put a tape of California bands on my stereo and got him a beer, but I didn't know what to do next.

Of course, if I told Mitch about how I made it with Spud of the French Fries, I'd practically have his pants off. But that would be shabby of me; you shouldn't kiss and tell, especially about switch-hitters or straight guys. Actually, I never did figure out Spud—he always liked to get sucked, but sometimes he liked to get fucked.

Spud had a great cock, the kind that starts out real thick at the base and then the shaft gets more narrow, and the cockhead almost comes to a point. It was great to suck that stiff boner while I played with his balls. Once I blew him right in the bathroom of a club right before he played a set. He said it relaxed him. And the times I fucked him, he liked to take it standing and bending over while I held his hips and drilled him. Man, that was hot.

Thinking about Spud got me horny, and I looked over at Mitch, who was talking about bands back in Ohio. His T-shirt was riding up over his stomach, and the sight of that smooth, tight belly was a turn-on. Just then the tape ended and I got an idea. I jumped up and popped in an old Tom Robinson tape, one that began with the song "Glad to be Gay." Then I stretched out on the carpet, closer to Mitch and almost in a sixty-nine position. At first he just heard the beat of the song, bobbing his head back and forth to it, and then he noticed the chorus...

Sing if you're glad to be gay...Sing if you're happy that way....

Right away, the Ohio kid caught the drift. I couldn't get used to those thick eyeglasses and those ET eyes, but I could tell he glanced over at me. In a matter of seconds, the idea of sex with a

16

guy went from the last thing on his mind to the first.

My face was no less than a foot from his basket, and there was no doubt he was getting one of those instant teen boners. I didn't waste any more time talking. It was time for me to make my move or forget it.

I dove right in, chewing the denim of his jeans where it covered his cock and massaging his balls with my hand. Mitch had his chance right there to push me away or tell me to quit, but instead I felt his shaft harden against my love bites.

Since Mitch was giving me the green light, I kept right on going. I opened his jeans and gave them and his white briefs a tug. His cock stood up, hard and ready, and it was the prettiest sight I'd seen in weeks. Most of the time you don't get what you want, so when you finally have it, you ought to enjoy it.

I wrapped a hand around his pretty, peach-fuzzed balls, then I wrapped my lips around his bone-hard cock. It was nearly seven inches long and about average width, and it was a rosy pink, just perfect for the blushing color of his smooth body.

I pushed up his T-shirt so I could look at his tight, hairless belly. Then I opened my own jeans to free my hard cock and play with it.

Mitch grabbed for my rod and his hand replaced mine. He stroked my bigger, thicker cock slowly, experimentally. We were still on the carpet, in a good position for a sixty-nine, but I didn't want to push it. I was bigger and older than he was, and if I just shoved my cock at him he would have gone down on it. But if somebody doesn't really want to suck a cock, he's not going to do a good job anyway. I can find plenty of guys who will give me good head when I want it. Finding a butch young punker like Mitch and

17

getting into his pants, now that was a real treat.

Pretty soon Mitch got the idea. No one was going to force him to do anything, and he could relax and just enjoy getting his cock sucked. Once he understood that I was really into giving him head, he turned into a randy little devil. I'd say "cocky," but that goes without saying. After a while, he let go of my cock and leaned back on his elbows to watch me.

Aside from the color and velvety texture of his cock, the nicest thing about it was how hard it was, like a solid ivory horn. I sucked it a long time, and I started to wonder if he wanted to come—or just go. But then he said, "Let's move over to the bed."

I put a long tape on the stereo and opened a couple of cold beers. "Take off your pants. It's better that way," I suggested, and I slipped out of mine.

Now Mitch was stretched across my bed in nothing but his black T-shirt, and a hotter sight you'll never see. His thick lips smiled at me with a smile that was farm-boy shy and sweet on one side and a sex-master sneer on the other. I couldn't connect with his eyes, but I was learning to read all the expressions of his mouth.

Getting comfortable on the bed, I nestled down between his gold-dusted thighs, ready for some serious cocksucking. It's not as good when you're bending over someone's lap or when someone is trying to blow you from some weird angle. The maximum-pleasure blowjob happens when the cocksucker—whether in bed or on his knees—brings his mouth directly down on his prize, getting every inch of it while he fondles the other's balls and maybe plays with his own cock. That may be the "missionary position" of blowjobs, but there are reasons why some positions stay popular for thousands of years.

Now it was easy to enjoy all of Mitch's cock, and I did, while my fingers tantalized his sensitive balls. He lifted his butt off the bed, arching his hips at me, and I didn't miss a beat. My lips caressed his stiff, pink beauty from the sweet cockhead all the way down the shaft to the fragrant nest of fine pubic hair.

Maybe Mitch was an Ohio hayseed, but he was a quick learner. What he was feeling was great, and that was all he had to know; he wanted every bit of it. I bobbed up and down on his curving cock for another five, maybe ten minutes, as he continued to lift his hips and jab it up at me. Then I felt the tension in his legs and thighs as they pressed against me, and I knew I could bring him off right away. It would have been easy to back off and make it last longer, but I'd already been blowing him for a long time and now I wanted his come.

Suddenly his flat, taut abdomen slapped up against my face, and I knew he'd passed the point of no return. I didn't care about getting myself off. Instead I brought both hands under him and grabbed the velvety-smooth cheeks of his muscular little ass. His hot cream load gushed, and I massaged his perfect, firm buns as he hammered my mouth.

We might never see each other again, but for a long moment there we both saw stars and shared the most intense physical pleasure that two people can ever reach.

Slowly, Mitch's body sank back to the mattress, and I continued to work his cock, with less pressure. Since I was happy just sucking this butch punker's member, it was the perfect moment to bring myself off and finish our little date. But I had a feeling about Mitch. Whatever his sexuality was or might become, he was one of those rare people who could enjoy sex right down his spine and all the way to his toes, with no quibbles or hang-ups. His cock softened, relaxed, but I didn't think we were finished.

I looked up at him, resting my head on his firm belly, my hands draped over his thighs as I slowly ground my hard-on against the mattress. His head was thrown back on the pillow and turned away, his sweet mouth open, and the big silver cross earring was resting on his shoulder. His thick glasses were ajar, and I could see a closed eyelid with long, pretty eyelashes. His body, breathing deeply but silently under me, smelled fresh and young and sexy.

Finally he came around and leaned up on his elbows. I glanced at him and remembered the magnified eyes, so I reached for my beer and started to talk. "You've had blowjobs before," I said. "You seemed used to it."

"My girlfriend," he said, with a little smug pout, "but that was real good." Then, "You like to swallow it?"

"Yeah," I said simply, and I imagined some girl or woman or guy spitting out his come in some motel bathroom or behind some barn. Whatever part of the truth was getting through, he liked that I took him all the way, whether or not he respected me for it. His mouth curled into a half-sneer, half-smile, and I could tell he loved the mixed feeling. I guess I did too.

We talked about rock clubs and bands and sipped our beers, but he was still spread out on the bed, naked except for the black T-shirt, and I was still more or less between his legs, waiting. And then he started pulling on his half-hard cock.

Knowing that you probably won't see someone again is a powerful turn-on. You can forget about who you are and just enjoy whatever catches a spark between you. Mitch had stopped talking.

I watched his cock get fully hard as he stroked it, and I looked up to his face. His head was tilted to one side, the silver cross earring on his cheek, and his lips were curled in that sexual, taunting smile.

So, I helped myself to seconds, going down on that pretty cock while I played with his balls and brought myself close to coming. Once I looked up and said, "Why don't you take off your T-shirt?" I wanted to see him completely naked.

"Nah," Mitch said, bringing a hand to his big thick glasses as if to keep them in place. "I like to keep my glasses on. I got one eye that's kind of crossed. It's getting better."

I wanted to tell him it would get better, that I knew about corrective lenses, and that I thought he was beautiful. But that was too much talk. Instead, I pushed his black T-shirt up to expose his tight belly and most of his smooth chest. I kissed him all along his body and went back to his rock hard cock.

Mitch started humping a little, and I could tell he was going to come fast this time. With both hands, I grabbed his firm, sweet ass again, and I held on to those hot buns as he started pumping his cock at me. Spurts of punkjuice hit the roof of my mouth, and he twisted and turned under me. I sucked his stiff rod until the rest of his body finally relaxed. Then my instinct took over.

"Just let me try something," I said, and I grabbed him by the hips and turned him onto his stomach. Just that fast, I was lying over him, my long hard-on rubbing along the crack of his apricot-peach buns.

"I can't be fucked," he said in a tiny voice.

"Okay, I'm just playing," I said, but as I moved my thick shaft back and forth between his silky-smooth asscheeks, he began to relax. In this position, it was now obvious that I was bigger than

21

him in all ways. I caressed his shoulders and back. The expression on his mouth changed, and he licked his lips.

When Mitch bucked his virgin ass up at me a little, I tried to go all the way. I reached for a little lube and brought the head of my throbbing dick to his tight assring. Mitch bit his lip but didn't complain. But after some real good tries with my lubed rod, and prodding with my fingers, I knew it was a lost cause. If Mitch really wanted in his soul to get fucked, it would have helped, but I don't think he did.

Still, he was a good enough sport to offer his buttcheeks to me the way he did. It was fantastic to hump him that way, riding the hard mounds of his ass with my long, thick cock, holding him down as I fucked, pressing his smooth buttcheeks together to caress my raging prick. I started to shoot, sending a come missile up his back, then spewing shot after shot into the sweet valley of his ass.

I kissed him on the cheek, then got a towel to clean myself and him. Now the expression on his mouth was a different kind, sneering and smiling at himself—as if he'd really degraded himself this time—enjoying it, the way a no-good punk rocker should.

Since I figured we were done, I climbed back into my jeans. "We could still catch the last band at the bar," I said. Mitch nodded and slowly started to put on his pants.

The phone rang and I answered. It was a friend who calls any time of night or day. When I finally hung up, I walked back to the bed to find my socks.

That's when Mitch surprised me.

He was lying back on some pillows with his jeans open and his cock sticking out as he rubbed it into a hard-on. I smiled. I didn't want to wound his ego, but I thought I'd sucked enough cock for one night "After I come," I said, "it's hard for me to get into it"

That sensual young mouth leered at me. "You just start licking around. You'll get into it"

He had my number—even more than I did. After a few minutes his pants were off again, and I was giving him another blowjob. His pent-up smalltown needs matched up with my own needs, and that's all there was to it

He came pretty fast that time. Then we had another beer and talked a while, until we both knew we were ready for more. His sweet body and pretty cock had me hotter than ever, and we both liked how much the other wanted it That was the thing. I blew him a fourth time— with his pants on but pushed down to his thighs—and it took a while, but he came again.

No doubt that little punker was one of the strangest tricks I ever had. But you can't go by appearances. We gave each other a time that neither of us would forget. When I said good-bye to him in the hallway, and he gave me one last arrogant, punky smile, I could have gone down on him again right then and there.

The Boy on the Bike

It all started back in Sioux City, where I grew up.

All my friends hung out at The Pit, the local Harley shop. We'd hang around with the bikers and watch them clean their wheels in front of the shop. We'd check out the newest leather and all the latest riding gear that came in. And we'd hang out with Clem in the back and watch him work on the bikes.

Clem was in his thirties and was the head mechanic at The Pit, and he could break down a bike with his eyes closed. He'd let us hang out in the service bay with him after the garage closed, and let us hand him tools, or give him a rag when he needed one. I loved Clem because he didn't give us younger dudes a hard time, like the bikers who hung out front. And Clem had the kind of body I wanted to have when I grew up to be a man. He was tall and olive skinned, and he had the kind of tight musculature that you only see on a man who works with his hands.

Twice he gave me a ride on his big Harley Roadster. I still remember hanging on to him, my arms around his torso, my body pressed up against his big, V-shaped back. I could feel his muscles draw tight as he worked that bike around the curves of the two-lane back roads he took. And the low, throaty rumble of that big two-stroke sent vibrations right between my legs. I didn't even know I was into guys at that point, but I sure knew that I got a strange, exciting feeling being crammed up against Clem.

One night I went by The Pit around eight. Clem was going to bore out the cylinders on a 1250, and he said I could help him out. I went around to the back entrance like I always did after closing and walked in through the little office that had been added on to the service bay. The guy who worked in the office was named Tom—he was in his twenties and kept the books. I was surprised that the door leading through the service bay was only open a crack. I put my eye up to it, and I'll never forget what I saw.

There was Clem with his jeans down to his knees, leaning back on that Harley, sporting a hard-on that made my eighteen-year-old pride seem like a roll of Life Savers. And Tom was there too, kneeling in front of him. Clem held his huge, hard cock at its base, waving it back and forth, slapping it against Tom's cheeks, dragging it across his mouth.

"C'mon, pussyboy," Clem growled. "Keep your hands to yourself. You'd better work if you want my dick." I'd never heard Clem talk like that, but the more he talked dirty, the more Tom gasped and moaned.

"Please," Tom gasped, "let me have it." But Clem kept slapping Tom with it, teasing him, making him chase the big head of his waving wand.

As for me, I was stuck in my tracks. At first I just stared, because I'd never seen anything like it. I'd never seen Clem acting so boss, and I'd certainly never seen a guy chasing after another guy's dick. But soon my curiosity turned into horniness. I'd fooled around with some of the local girls, copped some tit, even gotten my hands up a couple of skirts. But it never felt like this. Watching Tom lunging for Clem's big manhood was getting me hot and worked up. I started clamping my legs together and touching the outline of my prick through my cutoffs.

Finally, Clem let Tom have it, holding down his big, thick cock to be serviced. And like a starved dog Tom went right for it. He clamped his lips around that huge dick and starting sucking away, taking in almost half of the big shaft. While he slobbered on that cock, he used one hand to play with Clem's big balls and the other to jack his own cock.

Meanwhile, I unbuttoned my cutoffs and my boner jumped out, all hot and red and begging for relief. Careful not to make a sound, I started stroking my stiff eight inches while I watched the action.

"Come on, work that mouth, miss," Clem commanded, as he fucked Tom's face mercilessly. What seemed so hot to me, if I can explain it, was the way Tom just took it and took it. Clem rested his palms on the bike for leverage as he jammed his dick down Tom's throat until his balls were hitting the guy's chin.

I nearly gave myself away as I pressed closer to the door. Clem grabbed Tom's head in his two hands and held him in place while he just fucked his throat, pounding away like he was about to shoot. And he was, because he suddenly groaned and let go of Tom, who then sucked even wilder than he had before. His mouth just worked that shooting cock, sucking down that whole shaft, all the way to the base, getting every drop of come as Clem fired his load. Meanwhile, my whole body stiffened as I shot my load into my hand, all the while trying to stay quiet.

Only when Clem finished shooting and relaxed back against the bike did Tom bring himself off. He kept his lips wrapped around Clem's cock, which was still rubber hard, and jerked off until he shot a big load, leaning forward and swallowing all of Clem's meat while he came.

I knew that was my clue to get the hell out of there.

Wiping my hand on an oily rag, I pulled up my cutoffs, stood up, and backed out of the place. Once I got out of there, I went up the street to the diner and hung out there long enough for a burger and fries. About a half hour later, I went back to the garage, and Clem was there alone, acting like his old, cool self. I tried to act cool too, but I couldn't forget what I saw. And a few times I snuck a look at Clem's big basket.

After that, I really knew what got me off. It was masculine guys, especially guys who were into bikes. Just the thought of a tough boy and his wheels got me going. The smell of those well-worn leggings, and the sound of leather on vinyl as his ass slid onto the seat, his legs hugging that gas tank, and the impression of his cock showing through the cowhide, pointing down his leg— that's the stuff that got me hot. I had a few of the usual small-town experiences—a couple of quickies in the drama club dressing room, and some great times with a guy on the track team—but I never really lived my fantasies until I moved to New York City and got an apartment on the Lower East Side.

My first six months in the big town I made out okay, but I never came close to finding the kind of guy who turned me on. During the day I worked in a garage on lower Broadway, and that suited me fine. And at night I'd check out the bars in my neighborhood. I met some hot-looking guys and had some good times, but something was missing.

When I'm out cruising, I like to wear my leather jacket with just a T-shirt underneath. That usually attracts cute young guys my age. Plenty of my tricks tell me I'm cute, too, but they know by my look and my bike-shop muscles that I'm the guy on top. I mean, sure, I do like to suck a hot cock if it's on a butch guy, but when it comes to fucking, my tricks sooner or later roll over on their bellies and take my hard dicking.

Some people tell me I fuck kind of rough—not that they're complaining. Well, I think maybe I got extra rough because I always wound up frustrated after some time in bed with one of these college-boy types. It was okay, it got me off, but I never found anything that made me as hot as I was that time in Clem's bike shop.

Leather was part of it. In the city, every wimp and stringy-haired girl had a leather jacket for weekend wear. That pissed me off. Leather belongs on a guy who can wear it, someone with muscle and balls and class, like Clem. A few times I picked up guys who happened to be wearing leather, too, and that turned me on at first. But once I had them in bed, I knew it didn't mean anything to them—it was just a jacket.

I had more than a jacket, of course. I had black leather slacks and boots. But I almost never wore the whole bit, because it made me stand out too much among the blue-jeans crowd.

Finally one night after I'd fucked a blond boy silly, he turned over in bed and said, "You know, Mr. Rough Stuff, you ought to check out the West Side bars, the leather joints. Like the Spike, on Eleventh Avenue. Oh, you'll see some sissies and daytime accountants in leather drag, but if you're patient you'll find some real leather guys too. Until you, just now, I never met anybody who fucked me as wildly as a biker I met there one night."

"Yeah?" I said. "And would it be cool for me to dress all in leather for this place?"

The blond nuzzled down between my legs and started kissing my cock, bringing it back to life. "Listen, Butch," he said, looking up at me before putting my cock back in his mouth, "if not you, who?"

That was all I had to hear. The next night before my day off work, I went the whole route. From the shower, I stepped into a black-cotton jockstrap—my only concession to comfort. Then I got into my tight leather slacks, and they were worn enough to show my cock real well. I slipped into a ripped black T-shirt which showed enough of my hard, smooth chest. Then my sharp-looking boots and the jacket. Looking in the mirror, I saw one butch looking chicken in leather. I used my hands to mess up my short black hair and the picture was perfect. At the regular East Village bars, they'd be fighting over my dick. But for once I wasn't going to settle for letting some collegiate type get me off. Now I was going to go to the West Side, looking my absolute hottest and try to find the kind of guy who turned me on.

Well, the Spike was my first stop, and even before going inside, I felt a pleasant stirring in my jock. Some heavy-duty bikes were parked outside, and there were a few biker dudes who looked like the real thing, even if they weren't exactly hot.

Inside, I found a big two-room bar that had a wall-to-wall macho man atmosphere. This turned me on more than anything I'd seen in New York in half a year. More than anything, it reminded me of Clem's garage, and suddenly I got the hottest flash of that time I saw Clem getting head from Tom after hours. I felt a little more of that sweet discomfort in my tight leather slacks.

Unfortunately, none of the guys in the Spike lived up to the promise of the place. There were big daddy bikers, the kind who seem proud of their big, solid, pork guts. They looked right in leather—the trouble is, I wouldn't want them to remove a thing. And there were lots of phonies, the guys who push papers during the day then dress up in leather drag at night. Not that a real butch stud couldn't work in an office for a living and then look natural and sexy in nighttime leather. But I didn't see anybody like that there.

I did see a couple of guys who were okay—studly guys in their thirties who were no beauties but had good bods and were butch. I suppose I could've gotten into something like that, but no one really caught my eye. And I couldn't really hang out for long because I had a couple of leather-dudes following me around. Not to be mean, but some guys are so unattractive that they figure they have nothing to lose by being pushy and obnoxious. They will follow you around a bar or a bathhouse all night long, which, of course, also hurts your chances of connecting with anyone else. Sooner or later you either have to drop the dude with a left or leave. Since I think violence should be applied to fagbashers only, I decided to split.

Outside the night seemed alive and lusty—or was that just me? I knew there were other leather bars and back room clubs in the area, so I figured I'd take a little walk. I passed one place that looked like some kind of mixed leather and drag joint—too weird

30

for me. And another place looked okay from the outside, but when I got near the door I heard god-awful disco, so I knew it would be filled with leather wannabes.

Finally I saw a bar on a side street, and it had almost a dozen big bikes parked outside. This was either the real thing or as close as I was going to get.

Inside, I was surprised to see a small, square barroom with a pool table in the middle and nothing much happening. But right away I saw a number of butch-looking dudes in full leather. I strolled in and went up to the bar.

Sipping a beer, I glanced around at the guys playing pool or standing along the walls. Some were like the hotter guys I'd seen at the Spike, and some were sexier than that. Suddenly, I noticed the back room.

A curtain of heavy chains hung in an empty doorway, which lead to the darkened room in back. Well, I'd done enough standing around for one night—I made right for it.

Pushing aside the hanging chains, I stepped into a cavelike area that seemed as spacious as the front! The only light was a dim red one in a far corner, but when my eyes got used to it I could see plenty. And what I saw made my mouth drop open.

Most of the guys in the room, about a dozen of them, were crowded around a hot scene in the middle of the floor. I blinked my eyes over and over to make sure that what I was seeing was real—and it was. There was a stationary motorcycle, a beat-up old Harley, fixed upright on the cement floor, and on top of it was a naked guy who was getting it from both ends! Seeing is believing. He was hunched over, getting fucked in the butt while at the same time he leaned over the chrome handlebar to suck the big dick

31

hanging in front of him.

My heart was beating a mile a minute, the way it had in Clem's garage, as I stepped forward to get a better look. The guy on the bike was hot enough, about thirty and built solid. The cycle was held in place by some kind of iron mount, and on the floor next to it were the guy's boots and leather. The stud doing the fucking was older, about forty but a real bruiser, and his dick was a real ass rammer. He held the naked guy by the hips and banged him silly. The one in front, getting head, was tall and scrawny, but no sissy. His cock had a slim shaft, though it was really long and the guy on the bike could barely get his mouth halfway down its length.

This was a hot scene, watching that bull-dick pounding ass with the fuckee handling a mouthful of cock at the same time. I stepped forward a little, then jumped back as someone's hand grabbed my crotch. I didn't mean to be a prude, but it caught me off guard. Also, I'll let anyone cop a feel, but I don't like it when somebody who turns you off tries to force his paws all over you. The same guy grabbed me again, and I let him take one last squeeze of my basket, then stepped away.

When I looked back to the fuck action on the old cycle, my eyes had really adjusted to the dark, and I saw something a lot hotter. Past the hot threesome and the crazed pack of voyeurs, in a far corner of the cave-like room, I saw somebody so knockout gorgeous and sexy that my knees shook. Everything else stopped, and even the sex-pack in the center of the room became like a cardboard background.

Feeling brave and knowing that I looked as hot as I'm ever going to look in this lifetime, I walked around all the others and stepped right up to the young stud in the corner. He was wearing a leather jacket, a ripped T-shirt, and some kind of leather slacks or leggings. As I got closer, he gave me a hard look at first, then he gave me a half-nod, which meant, "Come on."

I stepped right up to him so that we were face-to-face. Fuck, he was beautiful. Really handsome with nice skin and short, sleek black hair. I figured that up close I'd discover he was about thirty, thirty-five, which would be fine, but no, he was only about my age. And while he was as tall as I and had the same kind of frame, he was really built. Not in a grotesque weightlifter way but with impressive solid muscle on his neck, shoulders, chest and arms, and all of that male power cutting away to a narrow waist.

They tell me I'm good looking, but this guy's face was so butch and handsome that I could hardly look at him. When I did, I was close enough to see that he had blue eyes. I ran a hand over his hard, smooth chest, and down his tight-muscled belly to his belt. He kept his hands at his sides and just looked back at me, waiting. And I could feel my face turn red when I realized what he was waiting for. He wanted me to get down on my knees and service his dick. And with those other men around! I felt freaked and kind of confused. I took a step back.

Every time I looked him in the eyes, my knees practically gave away, but I didn't want to lose this standoff. Who wanted who more? Well, I knew that it was only once in a blue moon that I found a guy whose dick I wanted to suck as much as this beautiful leather boy's. But I wanted to talk to him, to try to get him to go to my place or his place. And then it struck me: Who was being a pussy now? I was acting like one of these perfumed college boys, worried about the romantic setting.

The standoff ended as soon as the hot hunk got impatient

33

and started to move away. Like the first cock-crazed faggot from ancient times, I threw up a hand to stop him from leaving. Then, as he fixed me with a hard stare, I sank to my knees on the dirty concrete floor.

All of the world for me now came down to that basket in front of my face. I could see, outlined in the leather, a fat dick pressed down against enormous balls. I never saw leather slacks exactly like his before, but I unzipped the leggings enough to free his thick half-hard dick, and I lifted it away from those big balls so that it hung right in front of me. That hot, heavy slab hardened within seconds, curving up and thickening, inches from my mouth. I got my lips around it, and as soon as I tasted that dick, my own rod stiffened like lead in my own leather slacks.

My mouth took in as much of that fat shaft as possible while my hands fumbled with his belt. As fast as I could, I opened my slacks and freed my bone-hard dick. Then the young leather god did something with his leggings and leather gear—undid a few snaps, unzippered another zipper—and gave his slacks a shove down to his powerful thighs. Now his huge dick and juicy balls were completely exposed in front of me. The smell of leather, and the steam of his hot young flesh, drove me nuts. I ran one hand up under his T-shirt and felt the hard, smooth flesh of his abdomen, belly, and chest. I clamped my other hand around his balls and was surprised at the contrast of his hair with his upper body—his pitch black pubic hair was fragrant and silky, but it hung kind of long and luxuriant off his balls. I liked the natural feel and scent of it.

"Suck it," he said under his breath, and he shoved his hips out at me while grabbing the back of my head, driving that cock past

34

my tonsils and into my throat. Even though I couldn't breathe, I gave him my best shot, sliding my lips down that wide shaft till they hit the base and I had his iron-hard cock all the way down. Getting no air for a full minute or more, I just deep-throated him like that, sliding it back and forth, massaging it with the walls of my gullet. He groaned and held my head.

I heard some footsteps around us. The action on the motorcycle was over, and now a few of the voyeurs crowded around to watch this show. Fuck. I could tell my guy pushed off a few hands that tried to get a feel of his chest, then his balls. With him, no one would try twice. Somebody got down on his elbows under me, trying to get at my cock. I saw it was the one who'd been fucked from both ends, and I let him have it. His hot lips didn't do any harm, and it freed my other hand to stroke and worship the leather boy.

I sometimes go months without a chance to suck a cock, just because I never meet anyone hot and butch enough to turn me on that way. So, maybe I was rusty at first, but once I got into it, I was really sucking like I realized this was the hottest guy I'd ever blow. I fondled his balls with one hand and held onto his muscular right thigh with the other. I leaned into him and sucked that cock faster and faster, taking it all the way on each slide, and with both hands he lightly held my head, making sure I didn't even think about stopping.

Suddenly his cock seemed to harden and thicken even more, and he grabbed my hair and started pounding me with his rod. I felt hot come pelting the back of my throat, and I swallowed as best I could as he held me tight and kept fucking my face. In that moment my mind flashed on Clem and Tom in the garage.

35

It was kind of a white flash that was better than any orgasm, and for those couple of seconds I was right there, totally pliant, totally giving myself up to somebody and something that turned me on more than I'd ever understand.

In fact, I hadn't come. The guy who'd been sucking my dick got off when things got out of control, and then everyone else seemed to move away now that the action was over. I just stayed where I was, still sucking that fantastic dick before it started to soften. My red-hot cock was aching for release, and I thought of jerking off with this dream dick in my mouth. But I was hoping for something more—maybe that he'd jerk me off while I kissed him or something.

I got off that dick and off my knees, leaning on my wobbly legs against the lusty studling. Our hard bodies pressing together like that almost made me pass out.

Sure enough, he planted a kiss on my lips—his lips were thick and sexy, naturally. And he wrapped one hand around my pulsing dick.

Nobody else was in the back room now. From the other side of the iron-chain curtain, we heard some kind of cowbell clang in the front barroom for last call. These hardened barflies dig their sex games, but don't try to keep them from last call.

So at least we had a few minutes together. His blue eyes looked right into mine and his fingers stroked my hard-on. Make me come, is what my mind screamed. But my mouth blurted something far more mushy. "Don't fucking disappear," I said. "I really want to see you again." His body against mine was making me even crazier than his cock had.

The butch young leather god grinned and pushed me off. His

36

ass bared, he walked the five or so steps over to the stationary motorcycle and climbed on. Not understanding, I walked over, my hard dick swaying.

"C'mon," he said, bucking his hot, muscular ass up at me as he leaned down on the handlebars. "If you're man enough, it's yours. And, buddy, I don't give this ass to anyone except just the right person."

Feeling something like the balm of heaven wash over me, I laughed and said, "That's how I feel about my mouth, butch, and I gave it to you, right?"

He laughed. "Yeah, you gave it to me, cocksucker." Bending down to reach his pocket, which gave me an even better look at that muscled butt, he dropped a rubber and a little packet of lube on the floor.

Reaching for the protection, I saddled up on the bike seat behind him. The cycle was perfectly stationary and just the right height so that I could plant my boots on the floor while I fucked his ass.

I rubbered up and lubed his tight butthole. Then I massaged his hard asscheeks while I aimed my stiff rod at his target. He looked over his shoulder and taunted me in a low husky voice, "You moaned like a little girl while you sucked my dick. I thought you should know."

I laughed. "Yeah, well now your boy-pussy belongs to me. You're gonna be split and singing in a minute." In the dark I saw his flash of teeth as he held back a grin. He turned his face away and leaned down.

Inching into him slowly, I felt my hard dick poke through his tight hole. I ran my hands up and down his hard torso under his

T-shirt and felt the sweat breaking out over his hot, smooth flesh. He'd had me where he'd wanted me when I was on my knees, but now we were in my ballpark. I paused to give him time to get used to it. Then I started sliding the rest of my cock into him.

"Oh, god," he groaned, as low as he could, "fuck me, fuck me good." My hands settled on his hips, my thumbs rubbing the flank of his rounded ass-muscle. My dick was all the way inside him. I slid back slowly, to the ridge of the crown, then I drove it in harder. He gasped. I started sliding it back and forth at a regular fuck pace, and his hot butthole massaged me like velvet. His boots were on the bike's footrests, and his ass was all the way off the seat, surrendering to me totally. He was breathing kind of raspy, really into it.

Usually I never do shit like this, but I leaned forward and whispered in his ear, "Are you my little girlie now?" His mouth tightened, but there was nothing he could do—he knew his ass belonged to me now. And we both knew he'd probably pay me back later with a merciless face-fucking.

After holding back for so long, there was no way to put off my own release anymore. But I made the most of it. I held him in a viselike grip and stood all the way up as I pounded his ass. When I reached the point of no return, I was surprised at how long it went on, maybe because my aching balls had been ready to blast for so long. For perhaps a full minute, I fucked as hard as I could, faster and faster, my balls slapping his, as he leaned down over the handlebars and moaned as quietly as he could. The last thing he wanted was for those voyeurs to come back and watch him getting his tail banged—although he hadn't minded them watching me suck dick. This whole ping-pang, yin-yang, butch-butcher thing with him was turning me on like nothing ever did before.

I saw stars while I blasted, pounding away at the quivering ass of the boy on the bike. I came and came, and then kept fucking even after my balls were drained.

Finally I slowly pulled it out, and we both sat down on the leather seat. I wrapped my arms around him and held him as we both tried to catch our breath.

"You fucked my ass, you queer!" he said in a low, half-serious, half-teasing voice. "You're gonna pay for that."

I laughed. "I hope so," I said.

French Quarter Nights

I had wasted my first night in the French Quarter and I wanted to make up for lost time. I was twenty-seven, horny, and in New Orleans for the first time. True, I was there for a dumb business convention, but what I wanted was to party with Southern boys.

Still, I never got to the guy bars on that first night. I had a big dinner at Gallatois with some straight pals from my company. Then we'd walked along Bourbon Street, past Big Daddy's stripper club on our way to the Dixie music places. We went from one jazz club to another, until I drank half a dozen Hurricanes, and that's all I remember.

Now I was free. I'd gotten up well past noon, put on my suit and made one brief appearance at the business convention. I stood near the exhibit hall for half an hour, a good place to be seen by the people I worked with. After that, I knew I could skip the two days of seminars and go enjoy my all-expense-paid trip. By late afternoon I was in jeans and sneakers, checking out the gay bars.

I didn't get lucky right away. There were some nice looking

guys around, but they seemed more interested in playing pool or hanging out with each other. Maybe it was too early in the day for serious cruising. Or maybe I was being too fussy, as usual. At thirty, with a lean, solid build, good looks, and a thick nine-inch cock, I was always looking for the kind of knockouts I used to score during my chicken years. Sometimes I got them, but not as often. Of course, I should have been satisfied with sometimes, but that's human nature. We always want everything.

I was staying at a small gay guest house on Ursulines Avenue, away from the big hotels and my office buddies. After grabbing some dinner, I checked out the X-rated videos on the television in my room, and it was all I could do to keep from giving my hard dick some relief right there. But I figured I was bound to get lucky that night.

Hours later, I was glad I'd waited. Ignoring the routine bars I'd seen during the day, I went directly for the wildest place. Along a fifty-foot bar, five unbelievably hot boys in T-straps were dancing and accepting tips. A little too proud or shy, I couldn't bring myself to stuff money into one of those bulging, barely covered baskets, but I was blown away by the beauties who danced and swayed up above me.

I stood with dozens of other customers, holding my can of Dixie beer and lusting for the knockout bodies that were as sleek and smooth as any I'd ever seen. Long-haired and pretty, the dancers looked French, and down in New Orleans that made sense. All I knew was that I was getting turned on like crazy, but my frustration was growing. After all, I was at that awkward age. Though I had money to spare, I couldn't imagine actually offering to buy up one of these boys for the night, even though it

41

seemed clear that the hot young studs were taking offers. In fact, I believe there was even some low-rent quickie action going on in the dressing room in the back of the place. But me? Tall, dark, handsome, and hung me? Make an offer of cash for cock? On the other hand, what did I expect in that kind of place? Did I expect one of the working boys to suddenly see me and fall in love with me on the spot? I was definitely being dumb.

As the evening wore on, I was becoming more frustrated. A few times one of those mouth-watering beauties jumped off the bar and brushed right against me on his way to the back room or to join someone at a table. The press of a hot, hard, smooth, young body turned me on all the more. I knew I should either forget my pride and strike a bargain with one of these French Quarter cuties—like the long-haired blond who had me half-hard all night—or I should head out to one of the cruising bars and try to pick up someone. But I couldn't make up my mind.

A prisoner of both lust and pride, I found myself still at the stripper club when last call was announced. I knew some of the cruising bars were open all night, and I figured that was my next move. But my frustration had me thinking I would never get my rocks off that night. Undecided, I paused over my last drink while the dancers moved off to their dressing room. When one came out, dressed, and left with one of the customers, I knew it was time to leave.

Outside, I looked along Bourbon Street and weighed my options. Those blocks east of the cross section of Toulouse Street had some twenty-four hour gay places. But I'd already had five or six drinks. I didn't feel like standing around a cruise bar for an hour or two, drinking more. Even if I picked someone up, by that time I'd be asleep on my feet. I decided to go get a good night's sleep and try my luck the next day.

As I turned down Esplanade, I was surprised when a guy about my size and age stepped out of the shadows and stopped me. "Hi, I saw you inside," he said, trying to show that he was friendly. He was exactly my height, six feet, and dark haired, with a lean build. He had a handsome, not pretty, face. In other words, he wasn't the type I'd go after in a bar, but he wasn't bad by most peoples' scorecards.

"A pretty hot club," I said. I couldn't think what else to say. We were standing face-to-face under one of those gaslit lampposts. He was a regular guy, masculine, and he seemed kind of worked up after seeing those sexy dancers. So was I.

"Yeah. But it leaves you really horny," he said, embarrassed. I didn't say anything, but my mind was flashing ahead. Would I trick with this guy? He sort of reminded me of me. Before I could decide, he went out on a limb. He swallowed hard, looked around, then said, "I really like giving head."

"Sure, me too," I said, trying to assure him that I was gay, too, if he had any doubts.

"How about it?" he asked with a shy grin. And, since I was about to call the whole night a loss and just jerk off and go to sleep, I looked at him again, decided he wasn't a dangerous character, and nodded my head. That's how it works sometimes. You could spend hours and hours getting frustrated and pining to meet someone. Then, just like that, you could be strolling under the streetlamps, heading back to your hotel with a new friend.

My room had a little fridge that I'd stocked with beer, so we were able to have a nightcap as we talked. I pulled off my sneakers and socks and relaxed on the bed, and Billy—that was his name—sat on the end. We talked about the usual things, getting to know each other, and meanwhile I clicked on the television and one of the porn video selections.

Almost a half hour went by, and we talked and had another beer and watched some of the hot scenes in the video. I wasn't wildly turned on by Billy, but he was okay. He looked like a basketball player and was totally masculine, but I knew I'd have to make the first move. He was shy, or passive, whatever. Which made me realize how horny he was when he'd worked up the nerve to approach me on the street. Even more horny and frustrated than I was! Now that—the idea of his helpless lust—turned me on, and I could feel my cock start to come alive.

Just then, Billy went to the bathroom and I knew what to do. I pulled off my shirt and threw off my jeans. Since I don't wear underwear, I was naked and ready just like that. To be cool, I pulled the sheet just over my cock. But at the same time I took hold of my half-hard shaft and started pulling on it, getting it ready for him.

The bathroom door swung open and Billy looked at me with a grateful smile. "I thought you'd never do that," he said. Under the sheet, my rod was now fully hard and waiting.

He kicked off his sneakers and climbed onto the bottom of the bed without getting undressed. Not wanting to wait any more, he positioned himself between my legs, pulled the sheet down, and looked in awe at my cock. Not that it's the biggest cock you'll ever see. It's just a true nine inches—not a "gay nine," which comes in at around six. It's a real nine—thick, nicely colored along the shaft, with a beautifully shaped head. Now, me, I like different kinds of sex with different kinds of people. But I've found that true-blue, hard-core cocksuckers lick their lips over my boner. "Aw, fuck, it's great," Billy said, holding my hard-on in one hand.

That was the last thing he was able to say for a long time. His lips surrounded my shaft just below the crown and started sinking to the base with slow, hot mouthfuls. While both his hands played with my balls, his mouth moved up and down my cock, his suck action and caressing lips sending shivers up and down my spine.

Keeping one of his hands clamped around my balls, he brought the other one under me and grabbed at my asscheeks, not so much lusting for my buns as encouraging me to hump up at him. I began moving my hips faster; then I took hold of his head and started to give him a good face-fucking. And he had no problem handling my big, thrusting dick. But after a few minutes of that, Billy grabbed my hands and pushed them off. He didn't want me to get off right away; he wanted to make it last.

I relaxed back on my pillows and watched him. My cock swelled and throbbed even more as I watched it disappear into his face. He was into sucking slow and easy and really working his lips over every inch of my stiff shaft. I suppose I was used to getting or giving frenzied blowjobs, and now I was getting what the kids in my school days used to call an "S.B.J"—though I doubt any of them ever found out what a slow blowjob really felt like. Now I was finding out, and from one of the best cocksuckers I'd ever known.

My cock never looked bigger or harder, and it made me appreciate Billy's talented lips all the more. He wanted it to last so I didn't try to face-fuck him anymore. But every now and then I couldn't resist jabbing it up at him, skewering his face with the hard inches he was so hungry for. A few times I grabbed his head

45

and pulled it down slowly and forcefully, impaling him with my cock column until it was buried all the way down his throat. Then I'd let go and he'd slowly come back up, his lips dragging along every inch of all that hot, stiff meat. He loved it.

After this went on for a long time, I noticed that Billy finally had his cock out of his pants and was slowly pulling on it. Sitting up a little more, I could see it was a nice one, long and very dark, and the fingers of his free hand were caressing it lightly. I figured I wouldn't mind some sixty-nine action with this guy—and if I got his clothes off, maybe I'd be able to fuck him. After all his fantastic cocksucking, my prong felt like it could push its way into the tightest buns. But when I reached down to touch his hot, pulsing cock, he very deliberately took my hand off. And I realized this guy's whole trip was just to slavishly worship cock. There didn't seem to be a thing wrong with his own body and rod, but all he wanted was to keep his mouth filled with dick.

I could dig it. As I fell back on the pillows, I just surrendered and let Billy do it his way. Maybe I was just his type and he'd been frustrated for weeks. Now he was making up for lost time. My prong was almost numb from his clamping lips, and it got as hard as a morning boner, but I was content to let him have his way. I even drifted in and out of sleep a few times.

When I noticed the first light coming through the window shutters, I wasn't surprised, but I avoided looking at the clock. Finally, Billy must have gotten lockjaw from all that dick diving, because all of a sudden he changed his pace. He fondled my balls in a way that made me tingle all over, and he started sucking faster, harder, as if he were suddenly starved for the come load he'd been warming up for hours.

Again I noticed how talented this dick worshipper was. After holding back my load for so long, I thought I'd never get off until I got a few hours' sleep, but now Billy was pushing all the right buttons. My whole body tensed, my balls tightened, and suddenly there it was! My hips thrust up and I fired a big volley of cockcream into his mouth. I looked down to see him pistoning wildly up and down my straining rod as burst after burst of come splashed into his throat and filled his mouth.

Grabbing his shoulders, I held him right there to finish the job he'd started, and for a long time he bobbed up and down on that rock-hard cock, making sure he got every drop.

I fell back, exhausted, and gave myself up to sleep. But before I drifted away, I was aware of Billy beating off as fast as he could, while still wrapping his lips around my cock.

After that kind of treatment, I fell into a deep, dark sleep and didn't wake until well past noon. You won't need two guesses to know how I woke up.

Still dressed, still hunched at the bottom of the bed between my legs, Billy was working my revived dick. But this time he was using his quickie pace, determined to get my morning load as fast as possible. And since my rested cock was now sensitive again, he got it right away. I wasn't completely awake yet, and Billy was already helping himself to a Southern-style banana and cream breakfast. Deep-throating my cock for the last time, while he pounded his dick, he looked right up into my eyes just at the moment he shot his own load.

I showered while Billy merely splashed some water on his face. I never did get to see what his body was like. After dressing, I offered to take him out to lunch on my company expense account, but he said he had to get to work. Besides, after our long night of dick-in-throat action, I guess we had nothing much to say to each other.

I said good-bye to Billy on Chartres Street and watched him walk off, under some overhanging iron grillwork terraces, toward St. Louis Street. When he reached the corner he turned, waved, and was gone. It was hard to decide what to make of him, but I had to admit that he gave my cock an Olympic workout. I smiled, thinking that maybe his vacuum-action lips had stretched it an extra inch.

After a long lunch at a great cajun restaurant, I started walking slowly along Bourbon Street. The glaring late afternoon sun threw down a kind of penetrating heat I wasn't used to. New Orleans was a party town, but it was also the South, and I remembered that the climate was actually subtropical.

While the touristy section of Bourbon Street always seemed busy, the several blocks with gay bars were quiet in the daylight hours. The few people on the street walked in slow motion in the bright heat. A couple of obvious hustlers stood in doorways here and there, looking half-asleep as they waited around for a passing john. From a distance, these boys looked great: long-haired, young, and pretty, with the same French faces and bodies as the dancers I'd seen. But up close they seemed worn out, like they'd been partying too hard for too long. It made me think twice about fantasizing over a particular type.

The Corral Bar, a two-story corner building with an overhanging terrace, looked inviting, and I went in.

After my eyes adjusted to the indoors, I got a beer at the bar and looked at the guys standing by the jukebox and around the corralled-in dance area.

I liked the crowd. There were maybe a dozen or so young men in their twenties and thirties, dressed in jeans and T-shirts mostly. Regular guys, probably locals. And while no one seemed interested in cruising in midafternoon, I was ready just in case. I never wore underwear, and I had on my old jeans with the left pocket cut out. In cruisy situations I could discreetly reach in, give my cock a few tugs, and then give my prey an eyeful. It works—try it some time. Of course, the more you have to show the better it works.

Since no one really caught my attention, I climbed the narrow wooden stairway that led to the upper floor. Upstairs, a pool table filled the center of the small room, and there was a game in progress. One of the players was a dark, handsome guy in his thirties, and he nodded at me, then sank a ball while his friends watched. He wasn't exactly my type, but I was starting to wonder what my type was, anyway. Those French-looking street boys were my type, but at thirty I was starting to get tired of kids who were fucked up or trouble.

On the far side of the room, bright light poured in from the open double doors of the terrace. After watching the game for a few minutes I went outside. No one else was out there. I was standing on an uneven wooden terrace with a matching rail around it. I took one of the chairs and pulled it into a shady spot, then relaxed, watching the street.

Looking three or four blocks down Bourbon in the direction of the tourist action, I could see lots of people on the streets. But right below me the street was dead, with only an occasional passing car or pedestrian. And in the direction I came from, I could still see a few of those boys-of-the-night, looking kind of haggard in the day.

Lazy from the great meal and the quiet and heat, I went into a kind of trance. Then I heard the distinct sound of footsteps in the middle of the street. I was almost too lazy to look, but when I did I saw a short, very cute young guy crossing the intersection. The terrace hung so close to the street that I got a good look at him. He was about five foot nine, with a very hot body, and he was dressed in a blue work shirt, faded jeans and low construction boots. When I saw him heading right for the street door of the bar, I watched him more closely until he disappeared under the terrace.

That woke me up. He was a hot boy without being a pretty boy, and he wasn't dressed for disco but for work. I didn't know if he'd be interested in me, and maybe he was just stopping in for a quick beer or to meet a friend, but it was nice to see somebody I definitely liked. And when I gave my basket a squeeze, I could see that more than my interest was being stirred.

Trying to be cool, I decided to make myself wait before I strolled into the bar to check out this hot young thing. I even started counting, sixty seconds to the minute, so that I'd stay in my terrace chair for five full minutes. But before I finished counting I had the nicest surprise I've ever had in any cruising situation. I heard someone behind me and turned to see the kid, with two cans of cold beer in one hand, step out onto the terrace.

"Hi," he said, putting out his free hand to shake as he sat down in a chair next to me. "My name's Paul." He had a round smiling face, short brown hair, and one of those wispy, baby mustaches that young guys wear before they have to shave every day. He handed me one of the cold cans, grinning at himself for being so bold. "I saw you from the street," Paul said in a honeyed, soft voice, "and you looked real alone out here."

50

I told him my name and we talked for a while. He seemed interested in me because I was from up North and worked for a big company, and he liked that I was older than him. I took one look at the smooth, rounded chest that showed through his open work shirt, and I couldn't think of anything but getting his clothes off. Paul was twenty-one and a runaway from a town in Georgia. He worked five days a week on an oil rig, living out there with a bunch of rough men in a barracks type of atmosphere. But he didn't have any hot stories to tell.

"So far, no one's ever come on to me out there," he said, nodding in the direction of the Gulf. It took me a few minutes to get used to his accent, especially the way the words were drawn out. "I wouldn't mind. There's some hot men out on the rig, but I have to be careful. It's a good job and I don't want to lose it. But when I come in for my two days off, I'm always looking for fun. I can always stay at a friend's apartment where I keep my stuff, but I like to meet guys whenever I can. You got a room near here?"

"You bet," I said. We finished our beers and walked inside, past the pool table, and down the narrow stairs. While we were close together on the dark stairway, hidden from anyone else's view, I stopped and he bumped into me. I said, "Paul, put your hand in this pocket."

Of course, it was the pocket that was cut out, and my cock was thickened up and rubbery hard just from my being turned on by this little butch thing. He looked up at me with a grin as he slid his small, callused hand into the cut-out pocket and closed his hot fingers around my piece. Giving it a nice squeeze, he whistled through his teeth. Standing beside him, I noticed that he was about four inches shorter. Not my ideal type, but when someone's got a hold of your cock, he suddenly becomes exactly your type.

We kept going, out into the sun and along the few blocks to my guest house. "Great room," Paul said, getting out of his clothes before I had a chance to lock the door.

Even at twenty-one, he had one of the most hairless bodies I'd ever seen. He was completely naked while I was just starting to undress. His body didn't have an ounce of fat on it—he had a small, rounded and compact musculature, and that smooth, creamy skin. He stood there like that, waiting for me. His hard cock stuck out from his sparse, silky pubes. It wasn't more than six inches, but it was pretty and pointed and looked great on his lithe body.

As I threw off the last of my clothes and walked toward him, Paul stepped up onto the large bed, his cock pointing right at my face. Without missing a beat, I took that hot young boner in my mouth and grabbed those fuzzy balls in one hand. His cock was stiff as a poker and real sensitive. He moaned and groaned while I sucked on it, from the narrow head all the way to the thick base, tickling his balls at the same time. To my surprise, his body smelled soapy clean, and I figured he'd taken a long shower before leaving the rig. I liked the prettiness and hunkiness of his man-child body hovering above me.

While I kept sucking Paul's sweet cock, I brought both hands up to grab his buns. Just as I figured, they were smooth and melon hard. Just the feel of them brought my rod up to full attention. Which caught Paul's attention. Putting his hands on my shoulders, he moved his hips back and pulled his cock out of my mouth. Then he dropped from a standing to a sitting position on the bed and stooped down to swallow half my cock in one gulp.

Right away I had renewed respect for the talents of Billy

from the night before. Paul was not a great cocksucker. In fact, he seemed to have more teeth than a baby tiger shark. I could tell he'd told the truth about not getting any action out at the oil rig. But his excitement was a turn-on, and he held my balls with one hand while beating his hard poker with the other. He couldn't take in more than half of my nine-inch pole, but he sure looked good trying. And I knew there was another way he could take it all.

When I could see he was about to come, I pushed my hips forward, thrusting my dick deeper into his face at just the right moment. His spunk shot straight up, hitting his smooth chest and torso. I gave him another minute to hang on my hard-on, then I made my move.

Grabbing Paul under the arms, I pushed him back across the bed, then took him by the waist and turned him over. He was like a miniature statue toppled—that's how perfect his rounded muscular body seemed. He looked over his shoulder at me, a little scared and very excited. It was all there in his eyes: I was the tall oil rig worker who was sick of Paul looking at me in the showers, and now I was going to give him what he had coming.

Looking at his honeydew-melon buns, I felt that one of my wildest fantasies was coming true. You don't see such a muscular, solid little ass often, and usually it's in your dreams. Kneeling over him on the bed, I gripped his buttcheeks and bent down to take bites of that fresh young flesh. His ass was all mine, and I was letting him know it. But could I get past those golden gates?

An optimist, I always keep some lube and rubbers under my bed whenever I travel. While I held Paul down with one hand, I lubed up his tight, pink pucker with the other. This was not going to be easy, I could tell, as I wedged two fingers into his tight tunnel.

53

But the way he pushed his delectable butt up at me, I knew he was more than willing. I slid a rubber on.

Climbing right above him, I positioned my cockhead against his pliant porthole and gave a little push. A hard-on with any bend in it would have a hard time with such a squeaky-tight butthole, but his toothy cocksucking and the sight of his butch little body had gotten my rod as hard as a lead pipe. Paul gasped as my thick shaft made its way into him.

Since he failed to take my dick down his throat, I was going to make sure he took all of it up his ass. But one step at a time. Once I had a couple of inches imbedded in him, Paul stiffened up like he'd been harpooned. I held still for a minute, massaging his shoulders and back while I held him in place. Then I started moving my cock in and out, slowly sinking it deeper and deeper in the warm oven between those dreamy buns.

Though I don't like rubbers much, for once I was glad to have that slight, sensation-dulling effect. My thick shaft made its way into the tight chute, claiming inch after inch, without taking me to the brink of coming. Paul moaned and groaned, but soon he was working with me, pushing his ass up as I sank my rod down. Before long, we hit the perfect rhythm, and I was drilling him all the way. Looking down, I watched every inch of my long dick disappear into that hot ass.

Now Paul was moaning so loudly that I worried about anyone hearing him. Then I remembered that I was in a notorious gay hotel—the sound of my chicken frying wouldn't bother anybody— it'd turn them on. So I really let him have it. Pounding away at his ass faster and faster, I felt my balls tighten as my fantasy-turned-reality peaked. I held his shoulders in a viselike grip and slammed all the way in just as I fired my load.

Paul bit down on a pillow as I kept pistoning away, my shooting cock ramming all the way into him over and over, his tight assring draining every drop of my hot come. I kept going, slow-fucking him for long, selfish minutes, then finally I pulled out and collapsed onto the bed.

Surprising me, Paul pulled the come-filled rubber off and stuffed my bloated, sensitive cock into his mouth, swallowing more dick than he'd done before. I felt something hot splash against my leg, and I realized he'd shot his second load. Maybe he didn't have lots of experience getting fucked, but it was obvious that's what got him hot.

Climbing up, Paul rested his whole body on top of mine. I could feel his heart pounding as he kissed me, and I wrapped my arms around his powerful, compact body and held him tight.

Music and street sounds of the Quarter drifted in my shuttered window, and I realized it was night. I'd take Paul out for an expensive dinner on my company expense account, then we'd come back and fuck for hours.

And when I left New Orleans the next day, I knew I'd leave behind all my old ideas about what was the right type for me. Just be patient, and the right type will find you.

Field of Dream Boats

As baseball coach at a small-town community college, I see a lot more hot bodies than hot prospects. The first time I saw Vinnie Corvada at our spring tryouts, I knew I was looking at both.

Vinnie was a solidly built five foot ten, and a lefty. We had a few oversized kids who could throw hard, but Vinnie was in a different league. The Dominican-born nineteen-year-old had a smooth, natural motion, great control, and his pitches hit the catcher's glove with a crack.

At thirty-five and with no other college jobs on the horizon, I thought of myself as Coach Closet Case. I liked looking at some of the young men, but I kept my fantasies a deep dark secret Still, when you see someone like Vinnie, it's hard to keep your cool. To make matters worse, we didn't have enough jerseys for all the guys trying out that day, and Vinnie didn't bring a T-shirt. Leaving his dress shirt in a locker, he threw off the mound bare chested, and the sight of his smooth and muscular brown torso nearly put me over the edge. Even a number of the macho young athletes seemed to be admiring his knockout body, though they'd never admit it. When you're a coach, you notice things like that, at least when you're a queer coach.

My salary at the suburban drive-in college was a notch below that of a supermarket bag boy, but there were other compensations. As I said, I'd never fooled around with my players, though most were of age. But after practice and games, in the guise of protecting our limited clean towel supply, I handed out towels as the young hunks emerged from the shower room. This meant standing in an outer room, just outside the communal showers, which assured that I would see every naked studling on his way in and out. What a job!

Now, unless you are more of an unrepentant perv than I am, you probably know that not every young body will turn you on. Especially if you belong to a gym, you know this is true. But there's something truer than words about the naked body. The golden, handsome WASP who turns you on in his fine clothes might turn out to have a permanently pale, uninteresting body, and a frail, thin-stemmed bit of cock. But the plain and soft-spoken guy you hardly notice in his clothes might have a substantial body of the same rosy hue as his cheeks, and a thick and beautiful slab of cock that looks ready and willing for any kind of attention.

After that first tryout, when Vinnie was among those who made the team, I waited nervously near the shower room, handing out towels and waiting for the dark-skinned demigod to arrive in the flesh. Since the locker room was also crowded with all the young guys who didn't make the team, I stood beside a mountain of folded towels and watched the busy procession of young male flesh. Some of the studs who couldn't make the team certainly did make it in other areas. Even though all the equipment was put away, there were plenty of bats and balls swinging around.

To make matters more interesting, I had picked for the team the first obviously gay kid who'd ever tried out. And when I say obvious, I mean to everyone. Not that he was fey, but this red-haired kid, Rickie, actually showed up in an ACT UP T-shirt and with a gold lambda earring in his right ear. The spunky little eighteen-year-old couldn't really hit, but he had great hands and I decided he'd make a good extra infielder.

Although this Rickie had made the team fair and square, it made me a little nervous. In past years there were some closet gay and bi kids, and I'm sure some of the straight boys experimented too, but it was all kept quiet. That's perfect for a closet-case coach like myself. But an openly gay player might cause some trouble in the locker room and draw attention to me. While I was thinking of this, young Rickie strode into the tile anteroom in his birthday suit

What a pretty, smooth, pink body this young man had! Even his small thatch of red pubic hair was as fine as the strawberry red hair on his head. Rickie was smiling from ear to ear, partly from making the team, partly from being around so many hot male bodies, and partly from knowing that his coach was queer! Oh, yeah, he knew all right. He gave me a big, knowing grin, and when he walked past me to the showers, he looked over his shoulder at just the right moment to catch me looking at his peachy ass. And what an ass it was—smooth as a melon and beautiful. My face probably turned beet red. When I do pursue young studs—strictly off campus—I go for dark-skinned hunks. But I have to admit that my new infielder was cute as a button. Still, I didn't want him to know his coach lusted for his sweet lithe ass!

58

Before I had time to regain my composure, who should saunter into the white-tiled room but Vinnie Corvada. Somehow he had looked bigger on the mound, maybe because he was in such command. On even ground, he was medium sized at best, but I was blown away by his brown body, from the chiseled chest to the rippled, washboard stomach, to the narrow hips, and on down to the prominent sex toys, framed by his wiry pubes. What caught my eye first were the balls—large and plump and brown. I just wanted to cup my hand around them and start kissing those Latino lovenuts. His much darker cock hung down soft and small over that big ballsac, but my instinct told me that, with a little help, it would measure up to a very impressive size.

Vinnie strutted past me into the showers. Corded muscles defined themselves along the rounded cheeks of his perfect ass. I almost fainted away into my pile of towels. What I did do was hold a towel in front of my tented workout slacks, hiding my hard-on from the procession of presumably innocent young athletes parading back and forth in the nude. Somehow I knew that this would be no ordinary season.

Maybe it was my vivid imagination, but there seemed to be an unusual amount of steam coming out of the crowded shower room after Vinnie walked in there. And what had happened to Rickie, I wondered. When Vinnie finally came out, my eyes went right to his almost-black cock which seemed to have grown to a much more lip-smacking size in the hot water. Of course, when I lifted my eyes from that delicious-looking tubesteak, I met Vinnie's look directly. He grinned knowingly as he took a towel and said, "Thanks, Coach."

No sooner had my new pitcher's golden buns disappeared to

the outer locker room than little Rickie finally came out of the showers. As luscious as his entire nude body looked, I couldn't miss what had happened to his cock. Creamy white with a pink head, it now swung before him more than half-hard. No doubt he'd seen plenty that he liked in the crowded showers, and my guess was that Vinnie topped the list. With an embarrassed smile, he practically grabbed a towel out of my hands and covered his telltale dick. Then he scampered off, giving me another glimpse of that baby-skin ass.

Luckily, the weekend always gave me a chance to work out my frustrations, and after getting my first look at Vinnie and Rickie, I really needed some relief. Driving fifty miles to the city, I treated myself to a long night of male strippers at a hot club, and then to a room at the nearby baths.

I guess it seems funny for someone who sees so many nude athletes to pay to watch strippers, but to me it's a real turn-on. That night, the dancers ranged from a pale, skinny kid with a big dick, to a runaway farm boy type with rawboned muscle, to a slick character with a serious gymnasium build. All of them knew they were hot, and they liked showing it off.

After the club, I got lucky at the baths. I keep in shape strictly through calisthenics, and my slim body is well honed. I wound up sixty-nining with a blond beefcake in his midtwenties. It was great pressing his clean-smelling big body up against me while I tried to swallow his hard, curving cock. By the time I got down to his golden pubes, his seven-incher was past my tonsils.

The strong stud fucked my face while sucking me off, and we came at about the same rime. I loved the way his cock got extra hard when he lost control and pounded my face. But I hardly got a taste of his boycream because he held my head and shot right down my gullet. Then I kept that big, throbbing cock in my mouth while he brought me off. Afterwards the big blond smoked a cigarette and told me he was an auto mechanic. I just said I was a teacher and left it at that. It was a typical trip to the city for me. Lots of closeted men from the three-state area did the same thing on weekends.

The baseball team was my real life, though, and I lived to be around my players. You just have to take my word that it's not all cock lust—I love the game and we were having a good, respectable season. Hot stuff Vinnie was our ace pitcher, and the redhead Rickie kept things interesting.

All the boys knew Rickie was gay, but it seemed that everybody was cool about it. Maybe Rickie just handled it right, and maybe times really are changing—even in my part of the country—but it amazed me. I was still Coach Closet Case, but I now was more curious and horny than ever.

Oh, some of the players teased Rickie, but it was good-natured stuff, and he gave it right back. But I noticed that quietly, without jokes, Rickie seemed to have the hots for Vinnie. I saw how he followed the Latino dreamboat to the showers, and how they talked during baseball practice. Vinnie was a gentleman, but he was very macho. Was he giving the cute little infielder a little?

Finally, near the end of the baseball season, fate stepped in and dragged me out of the closet by my randy balls. It was after a practice session that nearly half the team had skipped. After all, it was late in the year and we weren't going to make the league playoffs—at that point I was grateful that the guys showed up for the games.

As usual, I gave towels to the young hunks as they stepped out of the steamy showers. And I also gave smiles and longing looks to macho-stud Vinnie and sweet-assed Rickie. Lusting for those two very different beauties was taking a toll on me. Weekend trips to the hot spots no longer got rid of my frustration. I felt older than my years, and I was starting to think of moving to the city and finding a new job and an open lifestyle.

Long after the locker room emptied out, I dragged the rubber barrel filled with used towels to the small laundry room at the back of the gym. Usually I liked to read the sports pages at night while I washed and dried the towels alone in the quiet field house. But that night all I could do was fantasize about Vinnie standing over me and smacking my face with his dark, rock-hard cock. While I started to stroke my own rod, I also got a flash of Rickie, lying facedown in the middle of the baseball field while I fucked his creamy ass.

Just as I was pulling my hard cock from my loose running pants, I heard a sound from the lockers. Someone was out there. I paused for a moment, staring at the towels turning in the giant washer. Then I got up and quietly stepped out into the locker room. It was one of those times when I didn't even want to think what I was hoping for. Maybe someone had forgotten something and come back for it. But maybe...

I passed row after row of empty lockers. When I came to the last one, I decided to walk quietly down the next-to-last row—if anyone was in the back corner of the changing room, I'd see them before they saw me. Near the end of the aisle, I heard a voice from the other side of the lockers.

"Yeah, do it, baby," a soft, low voice purred. Holding my breath,

I stood still, not daring to make a sound, though my heart was pounding like a drum. From my weekend nights at the baths, I quickly recognized the sounds of a blowjob in progress. "Yeah" and "mmmm" and lip-smacking sucking noises brought my rod to a full hard-on. With the silence of a cat burglar, I slipped to my knees so that I could peek around the corner of the last locker. And there I saw my horny heart's desire.

Vinnie was standing, fully naked, with a huge hard-on sticking out in profile. I could only get small glimpses of that big, chocolate Dominican dick because pink-fleshed Rickie was on his knees, sucking cock like there was no tomorrow. What a sight! Vinnie grabbed a handful of the redhead's hair and starting moving his hips, jamming his cock down that willing throat. For a second I wondered if these guys were doing it together for the first time, but Rickie took that hard slab of cock so easily, and Vinnie fucked his face so well, that I knew the answer. No wonder these two came to every practice and hung out at the gym so often.

Even before I realized it, my stiff rod was out of my pants and in my hand. Pressed against the corner of the lockers, I watched as Vinnie slammed his thick dick in and out of Rickie's hot mouth. Rickie's vanilla cock was pointed to the ceiling, but the action was so hot and wild that he didn't have a chance to yank it; he could only hang on to his pal's muscular thighs for balance.

Then, just when he seemed ready to shoot, Vinnie pulled his cock out of those vacuum lips and spun Rickie around. Reaching into his locker, he came up with a condom and got it on while his friend got his ass in position for a pounding.

No doubt about it: These guys were going through a regular routine. Rickie bent over to offer his creamy cheeks, and Vinnie grabbed him by the hips and saddled right up. I nearly fell over as I strained to watch that long, solid slab of cock disappear between those choice buns. Rickie moaned and quivered while he took his buddy's rammer.

Inch by inch, that thick butt-banger sank into Rickie's rear until finally Vinnie's wiry pubic hair was scratching those pink cheeks. Slowly at first, then a little faster, the Dominican stud pulled his rod most of the way out, then sank it back in, his own ass muscles clenching in pleasure.

"Oh, Vinnie, give it to me," Rickie moaned, and as if someone had flipped a switch, Vinnie started fucking faster. His powerful hands held his friend tight, and his hips were moving back and forth in quick, hard thrusts. Rickie tightened a hand around his own cock and started jerking fast, probably trying to come at the same time.

This was the hottest thing I'd ever seen. Afraid to make a noise, I held my aching cock in hand and leaned out a little further from my hiding place. Luckily, the two fuck-angels were facing away from me. But I almost gave myself away with a gasp when Vinnie started to shoot.

Pounding away at that gorgeous ass with loud slapping noises, Vinnie stood up on his toes as his muscles tightened and his body hammered Rickie. His head flew back and his mouth opened with a sigh. I could tell Vinnie was coming by the way his stud-butt fucked with short, violent jabs. "Yeah, baby," he groaned. At the same time Rickie was shooting his own hot come onto the gray cement floor of the locker room.

Knowing the frenzied fuckers were just seconds away from returning to earth, I quickly stood and began to retreat. Before

I got out of that aisle of empty lockers, one of my running shoes made a loud squeak on the bare floor. But without looking back, I got away from the locker area and down the long hallway to the laundry room. Once inside, I dropped onto a folding chair and caught my breath. I'd gotten away with it. I'd seen the hottest fuck ever, and I knew I'd never forget it.

Unfortunately, I didn't have time to shoot my own load while I was watching my players bunny-fuck. My hardest rod in memory stood up and demanded attention. Closing my eyes, I jerked it slowly, while visualizing the hot scene all over again.

Lost in my mental replay of those young hunks fucking, I slowly realized the showers were running. Thinking of the sexy pair now in the shower room, I changed my fantasy to the present moment, imagining them pressing against each other under the hot water, kissing and getting excited all over again. When the showers stopped, I knew that the young lovers were ready to get dressed and leave. I returned to my mental image of them fucking behind the lockers and got ready to relieve my pent-up frustrations.

"Hiya, Coach," Vinnie said. I nearly jumped out of my skin. I shoved my rod back into my running pants, but it looked even more obscene there than it had in my hand. I looked up, and both Vinnie and Rickie were standing at the doorway wearing nothing but towels.

"We heard you before," Rickie said with a taunting grin. "You saw us, didn't ya?"

I started to deny it, to pretend they were wrong, but finally I opened my eyes to what was obvious. Rickie was looking at me with an expression of lust, his eyes glued to the huge bulge in my pants. And Vinnie had a crooked smile that was more than just a tease. I suddenly realized that maybe they actually wanted to fuck around with me. They were certainly legal, and no one had to know. If ever there was a time to get out of the closet...

When he saw me lick my lips, Rickie smiled. "You know, Coach, I've been thinking about getting fucked by you since the first day I made the team. And Vinnie here, he doesn't satisfy me any more." They both laughed, but to show he was serious about wanting me, Rickie dropped his towel to the floor and leaned over the large washing machine, offering me that peachy ass.

"Yeah, do it," Vinnie growled in that sexy voice of his, handing me the fresh rubber he held in one hand, while bringing his other hand to the front of his towel to grope himself. That did it for me.

Dropping my running pants, I stood up behind Rickie who looked over his shoulder at me and smiled. I put my hands on those unbelievably smooth buns and spread the cheeks, exposing the pink, hairless little pucker that Vinnie's fucking had loosened up for me. I got the well-lubed rubber over my aching hard-on and didn't waste another second. The head of my long, swollen rod nudged into the tight opening, and Rickie squirmed and gasped. Then I started shoving it home.

Rickie clung to the top of the washer as I held his hips and started to skewer him with my iron-hard, ready-to-burst boner. For long, shuddering moments I watched my smoldering, stiff cock slide in and out of his parted checks. Then I felt Vinnie standing close, watching just as intently. "Fuck him, Coach, fuck him good," he said.

I looked over at Vinnie, and he saw right away how much I wanted him, too. With a smile, he climbed up onto the giant washer, kneeling above Rickie's prostrate body and facing me. The towel was still tied around his waist, but I reached under it and felt his Dominican beauty. Not quite hard yet, it felt hot to my touch and ready for more action. His balls seemed reloaded too, and his thick, bristly pubic hair turned me on.

While slow-fucking Rickie, I lowered my head and wrapped my lips around Vinnie's incredible dick. Vinnie put one hand on the back of my neck as I sucked his delicious dark meat, and his shaft quickly expanded, thickened, and hardened in my mouth. His clean, male scent was so exciting that I stopped moving my cock in Rickie's ass so I wouldn't shoot off quite yet.

Vinnie pulled the towel away, and all I saw were those washboard abdominal muscles that I'd lusted over all season. Then I turned my eyes down to the hard column of cock in my mouth. Now he was practically sitting on Rickie's back and thrusting his hard pole up at me while he continued to hold me by the back of the neck. The macho stud knew how to take what he wanted, and his dick had me so turned on that he could have been as rough as he liked. No doubt he was used to getting his way.

Meanwhile, Rickie was too heated up to be teased, and he started riding his sweet ass back at me, impaling himself again and again on my overstimulated rod. I felt my balls rise with the first warning of an explosion. At the same time, Vinnie grabbed my hair and started forcing my head all the way down on his cock as he thrust it up at me. His cream filled my mouth, and I swallowed it madly as I started humping Rickie's hot ass faster and harder.

Both of Vinnie's hands held my head in place while I kept his spent cock in my mouth, my nose in his bristly aromatic pubes. I started firing bolts of hot come into Rickie's quivering ass, each thrust slamming him hard against the washing machine. After the long wait for release, my balls shot a full load into the trusty rubber.

The alarm on the nearby dryer went off and we all jumped, then laughed.

After we got untangled and I pulled the rubber off my sensitive cock, Rickie dropped to his knees in front of me and nursed my rock-hard dick with his velvety lips while he jerked himself off. I looked at his pretty cock as he shot off, and I knew I'd like to suck it some time real soon—maybe without Vinnie around.

As it turned out, I got more than my wish. Before the end of the semester, I had a few more threesomes with the sexy duo and a time alone with each of them. And that's why I'll never forget last season.

This season, Vinnie is pitching both the ball and his fantastic dick at another college, thanks to a baseball scholarship. But Rickie is still the shortstop on my field of dream boats, and after every game he helps me in the laundry room. Better yet, the little redhead is helping me out of the closet for keeps. Next season we're teaming up at a big university in the city.

Chinese Takeout

On nights when my boyfriend doesn't come by, I have to get dinner for myself. I tend to do whatever is lazy, easy, and convenient. One night, on my way home from work, I stopped at the local Chinese takeout joint.

The place was really a dump. The name was Hong Kong Kitchen and they only had three tables—in case anyone was crazy enough to eat there. But the food was actually okay, and I occasionally picked up dinner there. And I always got a kick out of the Chinese boy who took my order.

He was about twenty and very pretty, and he blushed when I talked to him. His baby face was round and sweet, and he had jet black hair and long eyelashes. He wasn't tall and scrawny like his two older brothers—who did all the preparation and cooking while he took orders and packaged the food. His smooth body was small and nicely rounded under his loose-fitting white uniform.

Best of all, his name was Chuu-Dong, which made me think of "chew dong," which is what I wanted him to do. When I heard one of his chef-brothers call him by name, I always looked up from my newspaper and glanced at the kid's pretty face and his large sensuous lips.

I ordered a safe dish, and Chuu-Dong looked up at me from across the counter and said, "Large or small, please?"

I wanted a small order, but I looked into his beautiful eyes and heard myself say, with a smile, "Large." The blush spread over his face and he looked down, but he was smiling. I didn't tease him after that because I sensed he was embarrassed in front of his brothers, who didn't seemed to be sensitive, thoughtful human beings.

Anyway, I had half a hard-on from being near him before I got my order and left. There didn't seem to be any way to get to know Chuu-Dong better, but I always got a kick out of seeing him and watching him blush. Usually he blushed any time I looked him in the eyes.

I don't know how my thing with Chinese boys and men got started. I had a regular boyfriend, twenty-seven and Irish, who stayed over at my place about half the time, and we had what you'd call an okay, average sex life. Naturally, I sometimes strayed. At thirty-five with a regular build, a handsome face, and a big dick, I'm not the sex-crazy kid I used to be—but I have to sneak in an occasional fling. That doesn't seem so wrong.

Anyway, after this last brush with the blushing boy, I ate my dinner alone at home and tried to remember how my secret fantasy for Chinese guys got started.

Maybe it was a few years earlier. I was at a local porn theater, the kind that has lots of backroom space. It's a charge just to walk through those places. If you're lucky, you can have a little safe fun

70

in the corner somewhere. I remember one night when I had my eye on a hot young dude. I just wanted to get together with his incredible, bulging basket. But suddenly someone else staked his claim on me.

It was in a large, dark area that was actually behind the theater's movie screen. About a dozen guys were cruising or fooling around. Suddenly this Chinese kid in his twenties walked right up to me, quickly looked into my eyes, and dropped to his knees. We weren't even off to one side—we were right in the middle of the floor. But he wanted it so much that it turned me on. I unzipped my jeans and brought out my fat, tumescent cock. The Chinese kid wasn't that attractive, but, as they say, everyone is beautiful with your cock in their mouth. The way he clamped his juicy lips on my rapidly stiffening rod made my knees buckle for a split second. And the way he looked up at me—as if this was the cock he'd always dreamed about—made my balls tingle.

Although I'm not an exhibitionist, I didn't care about the small crowd that had gathered around us. All that mattered was how good those hot, hungry lips felt sliding up and down my thick nine inches. He brought his mouth all the way to the ridge of my dickhead, running his tongue under it, then dove all the way down on the shaft, driving the head into his throat, burying his nose in the pubic hair that showed through my open zipper.

He gulped and gasped, sucking faster and faster, as if he thought I might pull out at any moment. But I opened the button on my jeans and shoved them partway down my thighs. I wasn't wearing underwear, so the Chinese kid now had a total view of the big dick that he was worshipping with his warm lips. He wrapped one hand around my balls and used the other one to grab onto my thigh to steady himself. If it weren't for all the groping onlookers, none of whom were much to look at, I would have dropped my jeans lower. But as it was, my starving cocksucker mumbled, "Mmtnphh," at the sight of my flat abdomen, nest of pubic hair, and the thick base of my cock which he was trying to reach with his lips on every downstroke.

Finally I grabbed his head, my fingers running into his jet black hair, and I held him steady while I started to mouth-fuck him, paying no attention to his sputtering gasps. He kept looking up at me, then back down at the long column of cock that was piston-fucking his mouth. He let go of my balls and started whacking his weenie at high speed so that we'd come at the same time. Electric charges jolted through my ass and up my back. The magic little trigger deep inside me snapped, and I held his head tighter as my hot torrent of come exploded in his mouth.

Only then did he actually take every inch of my long pole down his throat. As burst after burst of my load filled his chipmunk like cheeks, I let go of the kid's head and he fell forward, sliding his lips down to the very root of my rod. I realized he was coming at the same time that he held my swollen, throbbing cock in the depths of his satisfied gullet.

Then the crowd of horny onlookers turned away. I remembered where I was, and I was ready to get out. But the hungry kid on his knees wasn't ready to quit. He slowly, lovingly sucked on my long and rubbery-hard cock. He kept me there for another five to ten minutes.

Since then, I've had a number of hot times with Chinese guys. It wasn't always young ones; sometimes it was a man my own age or older. The one thing that made it special, I suppose, was the combination of a small Chinese guy and a big Caucasian cock. I realized it wouldn't be the same with a six-foot, hundred and eighty pound Chinese man. I still had all kinds of sex with all kinds of guys. But this one kinky thing, I don't know...it just gave me an extra charge.

My phone rang, breaking the spell of my sex-memories. It was my boyfriend. On nights when he didn't come over, we spoke to each other on the phone. I was glad to hear his voice. We made plans for the weekend. But as soon as I said good night and hung up, my horny thoughts came back in a rush.

I thought about pulling out a video and setting in for a nice jerk-off session. But somehow that didn't interest me. Then I realized that I wasn't interested because I didn't have a porn video with Chinese boys in it. The kid from Hong Kong Kitchen had really put the idea in my head.

Before I knew it, I was walking the ten blocks to the porn movie theater where I'd first gotten hooked on my secret fetish. While I walked, I wondered what made it such a turn-on. And I realized it was the fact that the other partner, the Chinese boy or man, was so turned on. Something about me, and maybe it was something more than just my big dick, turned *them* on like crazy.

At the movie theater, a cashier took my money, and in the time it takes you to walk through two doors, I left behind the bleak, violent streets of the straight world and found myself in the familiar, dark, sex-charged atmosphere. A couple of young guys standing in the back of the theater turned to check me out. I looked ahead, down a narrow, dark aisle to the big screen that showed two hot California blonds sixty-nining on a beach.

As my eyes adjusted, I could see that the theater was pretty empty. I took a quick walk down the aisle and back up. There were a couple of college-age kids sitting together, each with a hard-on sticking through his fly that was being handled by the other. I almost sat behind them. But I wasn't that outrageously horny, and they seemed kind of mushy, kissing and all. The other dozen people in the rows of seats are best forgotten.

So I returned to the front and scooted down a side staircase to the basement level, which had a small video screen and some cavelike back rooms.

One quick look through the dark back rooms was all I needed. There was some action, but no one that interested me. I did see one cute young guy sitting on one of the plastic chairs in front of the video screen, but he was fast asleep! Then I spotted the Chinese boy.

He was short, pretty, and, I'd guess, twenty-three. He was dressed in clean white slacks and a loose-fitting white cotton jacket. I stood ten feet from him and we both pretended to watch the movie screen. My dick began to come to life.

Almost every time I looked from the screen toward him, he was looking at me. Then he'd turn away. I was getting frustrated, and I sensed he was my best and maybe only shot at some action.

Finally, when no one else was walking through the video room, I slipped down the zipper of my jeans. With my hand hidden by my long leather jacket, I took out my half-hard cock and gave it a few tugs. Then I turned to the Chinese boy in the white suit.

He looked at my face, then down at the hard-on I showed him. His gaze was stuck on my length of thick dick, and I gave it a shake. It was like having a fish on a hook. He looked up at my face and licked his lips.

I wedged my cock into my open pants and walked the short distance to the nearest back room. It was a dark basement space. Hearing his footsteps behind me, I stood facing a dark corner and pulled out my throbber and stroked it He slipped in front of me, into the tight corner, and dropped to his knees.

He wasn't that good at sucking cock, but he gave it his best. I wrapped both hands around his head and started feeding it to him. The warmth of his small mouth made my dick thicken and stand up to its full length. Before long he stopped sucking and opened his mouth wider to take in all of my pulsing prong. The ache in my balls started to turn into something else. Somehow it turned me on even more to think of his clean white slacks on the dirty floor.

Even in the dark I could see his pretty face getting fucked so roughly by my angry, driving cock. His gasping and sputtering drew some guys over, and they looked around me, down at the face-fuck that was heating up. But I kept their groping hands away from the action.

The kid looked up at me and opened wider, taking as much of my rod into his mouth as possible. But that still wasn't much; not more than half of my stiff meat was getting in before banging into the back of his throat.

Finally the churning in my balls was too much, and I held him tighter and jammed all the way in, getting the shaft down his throat. Then I held his face against my pubes, his chin against my balls, and my load fired its way down his gullet When he gagged and pulled back, a second shot of come splattered across his pretty face. Quickly the kid leaned forward, grabbing my balls so I couldn't get away, and he deep-throated me on his own for the first time. I couldn't see much in the darkness, but I figured he was coming. Someone's hand was touching my ass, and I wanted to leave.

A few minutes more and I finally backed away from all the hands and bodies that pressed around me. I was halfway up the stairs to the exit before I got my zipper closed.

That adventure cooled me off and helped me behave for a few weeks. I got back into my steady routine with my boyfriend, who cooked dinners for me, brought me flowers, and gave me his sweet little butt whenever I wanted it. I knew I ought to be satisfied with such a relationship, but it's just human nature to want something extra.

I was on my way home one night, after a late day at work, just before I reached my house, two scrawny Chinese boys in ski jackets passed me on the street. I recognized them. They were Chuu-Dong's brothers, and they were walking away from the takeout restaurant. I backtracked up the street.

Sure enough, there was a CLOSED sign in the window—but the door was still unlocked. I opened it and walked in.

Chuu-Dong was on the other side of the counter, washing a large wok in the sink. He turned in surprise, but it was plain that he recognized me. He looked at me and he knew. He swallowed hard and reached over to shut off the faucet. I locked the door.

I went through the inner door to the other side of the counter and the kitchen. The pretty boy looked up at me, his eyes wide. It occurred to me that I was about a foot taller than him. I didn't know what to say, so I put my hands on his shoulders and rubbed them, then pulled him closer to me. His soft little hands rested on my basket, and he put his face against my chest. I swear he smelled like a bouquet of flowers.

I reached down and kissed him, and my hands were feeling his round, meaty butt. It was so quiet you could hear footsteps on the street and passing cars. But no one could see into the kitchen from the small front window. I held the pretty body and massaged his ass while he snuggled against me. "Chuu-Dong," I whispered, "I'm going to fuck your ass."

"What your name?" he asked me.

"Junior."

"You not hurt me, okay?" he said, not asking but sort of telling. I wondered who might have hurt him. I nodded.

Chuu-Dong started undressing, and I hesitated and then did the same. I figured he knew his brothers weren't coming back.

After he got his sneakers and socks off, he was naked in half a minute. He unbuttoned the loose white shirt and dropped it. There was nothing underneath. His well-proportioned chest was smooth and alabaster pale, with sexy brown dime-sized nipples. He unbuckled his white cotton slacks, and they dropped to the floor. He wasn't wearing underwear. His hard cock was very pretty, white with a pink head, and it pressed up against his taut boy-belly.

I took a little longer to get out of my clothes. My cock doesn't get instantly hard, but it was halfway there and Chuu-Dong caught his breath when he saw it.

I grabbed his sweet spring roll and slowly jerked it up and down while I tugged at his pink balls. His pubic hair was as fine as silk. He pressed his body against me, and his flesh was hot and satiny smooth. My dick really hardened then. Seeing it, he pulled free of me and dropped to the kitchen floor.

I looked down at that fine head of jet black hair, the long silky

77

lashes of his closed eyes, and those juicy, sensuous lips which were wrapped around my throbbing cock. He sucked so well, in long, moist, deliberate strokes, that my balls tightened and my ass clenched. But there was no way I wanted to come that way. Not this time.

With one hand he grabbed my balls and started to play with them. With the other, he grabbed his cock and started jerking it real fast. I used my bare foot to push his hand away from his rock-hard poker. I didn't want him to come right away either.

But I couldn't resist enjoying those luscious lips a little longer. I put my hands on both sides of his head and held him steady while I slowly brought my shaft in and out. His hot mouth caressed every inch, sending waves of pleasure through me. Then I felt myself getting close and I stopped him.

Lifting Chuu-Dong under the arms, I brought him up and kissed him again. When we separated he was breathing hard, and he licked his lips. I ran my hands down his perfectly proportioned little torso, then I grabbed him by the hips and turned him around.

His ass was as beautiful as I'd fantasized. Round like a girl's but firm like a boy's, and creamy white and smooth. I bent him over the woodblock table so that his toes barely touched the floor. I parted his almond-cookie cheeks with my hands and saw his hairless pink butthole quivering. First I used a little spit. But when I saw the container filled with packages of duck sauce, I couldn't resist

I opened two packets at once and rubbed the golden duck sauce on his tight pucker and also on my anxious dick. Then I held him tightly by his hunky little hips and started to work my way into his Chinese treasure. He gasped as the dickhead slid in.

Of course, I gave him time to adjust. But then I started to sink my shaft between those parted buns.

Moving my hips slowly back and forth, I gave him enough fuck-pleasure to smooth over the pain. While I gently fucked him, I gained inch after inch. When I got the whole length into him he buried his head in his folded arms and started saying things in Chinese.

The hot, tight, warm paradise was almost more than I could stand. He relaxed and gave himself to me. Then I started fucking for real, driving my hard shaft into him faster and faster while still holding him firmly by the hips.

Out of the stream of Chinese words he suddenly moaned, "Ahh, fuck, white boy, fuck!" It sounded like the loud purring of a cat. My balls started to tingle, my hair fell across my eyes, I was sweating, and my body was slapping against his voluptuous butt as I drilled him.

I picked up the pace. It was out-of-control time. Chuu-Dong's feet came off the floor as my fucking drove him up onto the woodblock table. There was a huge pile of bean sprouts on the clean tabletop and he was sliding into it.

I anchored my hands under him so that his balls wouldn't get hurt against the table. I grabbed his horn-hard dick and held it so that his wild fuck motions would whack him off at the same time. But he was way ahead of me; he moaned out loud as I felt his hot load gushing into my hand.

I shot a blast into him that felt like my first really good come charge in months. Then I sort of pulled him toward me with my arms, holding him off the table, suspended against me as my hard dick machine gun-fucked his beautiful ass. I slammed into him that way for I don't know how long, draining every drop of come from my balls.

Finally we were both completely fucked out. I lowered him back onto the table. His butch-baby arms were in the pile of bean sprouts, and he gasped to catch his breath.

When he could finally regain his balance, he hopped off the table and reached down for his clothes. He looked up at me again and smiled and blushed. That beautiful blush. I looked at his perfect body and I didn't want to get dressed.

"Chuu-Dong," I said, looking him in the eye, "I live two streets from here. Come home with me?"

"But I must clean now," he said, gesturing at the kitchen around us.

"I'll help you."

And soon we were both walking back to my place. I was taking out the takeout boy. I didn't know what would come of it. I still loved my boyfriend, but I'd think about that later. All those other Chinese boys made me realize that there was something locked inside me. And now Chuu-Dong had turned the key.

Lovers' Lane Action

I grew up in a real small town surrounded by hills and countryside. By the time I was twenty, I knew I was gay, but there wasn't much I could do to act on it. I hung out with the same crowd I graduated high school with, and in my town everybody knew everybody else's business. The few hot times I'd had with other guys were during weekend trips to Chicago. But when I got back home, there was no way I could satisfy my need for male sex. Until that weekend, when I discovered what went on at the local lovers' lane.

Oh, I knew guys and girls fooled around at lovers' lane, which was a parked-car overlook between two hills, half a mile outside of town. It was close to the drive-in movie theater, and a lot of guys would bring their dates there afterward. They'd sit in the car and lie about love and honor, usually for no more than a handful of ass and a hand job. Of course, to young horny guys in a Bible-Belt town, that was just fine.

Sure I knew about lovers' lane. Twice I'd even brought this girl Jenny there after a movie. I didn't mind kissing and playing with her a little, because I wound up getting my aching cock pulled off both times. But she wouldn't do more than pull and kiss it—no sucking for that Christian virgin—and to me that seemed a lot of trouble, plus the cost of movie tickets, for a job I could do better! Then I found out there was more to the lovers' lane action than I ever imagined.

One night I went to the drive-in with my friend Joey. It was a rock 'n'roll movie, and Joey was a tall, crewcut guitar player in a local band. If we'd been closer friends, I guess I would have told him the truth—that his guitar skills were not so great and his band was the pits. But I only hung out with Joey every now and then, and even though I had no hope of getting into his pants, I did have the hots for him.

Aside from his sexy, crewcut hair, Joey also had a cute face, a lewd grin, and a lean, lanky body. I used to fantasize about what his cock was like—I'd never seen it in the school gym shower room because he was a year younger than I and hadn't been in the same class. But we lived near each other, and I think my long, wild black hair made him assume I was a real rock 'n' roller like him.

Anyway, we watched a movie and shared a six-pack of beer in the front seat of his old car. I remember that the movie was boring, and Joey fell asleep after his third beer. This was murder for me, because my fantasies almost got away from me. I mean, here I was in the darkness of the parked car and Joey was fast asleep behind the wheel, his head thrown back and his legs spread wide.

The flickering light of the movie on the big screen came through the windshield of the car, and since Joey was asleep I was able to really look at him, and it made for a better show than the flick. Under his T-shirt and loose cotton slacks, his body didn't show an ounce of fat. Making sure he was really asleep, I took a good close-up look at his basket, but I can't say it showed much. Still, it showed enough—an inviting lump of cockmeat was surely there on the right side of his pants.

Well, I knew Joey, and I knew it would be a disaster to have him wake up with my head in his lap. So, I just sat there frustrated and watched the rest of the movie. Then I woke him up, and we started up the car and got out of there.

"Hey, I got an idea," said Joey, coming to life as we pulled out onto the highway heading back to town.

"Let's take a detour off to the lovers' lane. You know, park the car off to the side and sneak up and see what we can see. Sound like fun to you?"

"Yeah, sure," I said. I knew it could lead to more frustration, but just the idea of being in the woods, with Joey getting all horned up, turned me on. Maybe if we saw some couples making it, Joey would want to jerk off. I'd settle for getting a look at that dick, especially if we were both pounding away.

We parked under some trees and walked along on a gravel path, through the woods and up to where the lovers' lane overlook was. We still had a couple of half-quart cans of beer, and we took them with us. Sure enough, five cars were parked there, all of them discreetly spread out. We got down and crept up pretty close to the car nearest us. Some guy we knew was in there with his steady, and there was definitely action going on. The guy, a football jock from Joey's graduating class, had his bucket seat pushed all the way back in his little sports car. We got close enough to see his girl's head bobbing up and down. What we saw really was just the silhouette of this hetero blowjob, but it was pretty hot.

83

"Oh, man," said Joey, as we crouched down in the bushes, "that's getting me hot." Kneeling beside him, I could see him touching a hand to his basket. My own cock jumped up like a jack-in-the-box. Oh, please, god, I thought, please let him take it out. Then the couple in the car changed positions, and then all we could see was the jock's shoulders and head. He was on top of her, slow-fucking her. "Ohhhh," Joey groaned, sounding like he was in pain.

I thought for sure he'd be pulling out his rod any second, that we'd be jerking off side by side in the moonlight. It never occurred to me that I could initiate something, that I might pull out my cock and encourage him to do the same. Of course not—like any gay boy before coming out, I was afraid of being called "queer." Years later, I'd realize that young straight guys did the queerest things all the time, but somehow that was okay. So, I waited for Joey to do something, but no such luck. He stood up suddenly, leading me back to the gravel path heading toward the car.

"Fuck," he said, "we can't get any closer without getting caught, and it's just making me horny as hell. Hey, look down there!" He was pointing to a part of the woods down below the lovers' lane, a few acres of clearing that had lots of shrubs and a dozen or so trees. "See on the other side of that ravine, those parked cars?"

I could see several cars parked in the dark, off the main road. "What is it? More couples down there?" I asked.

"No, man," Joey said, "that is Gayville, USA. Mark Hamilton, the basketball captain of this year's senior class, told me all about it. He said these gay guys from other towns, mostly from the college at Kenosha, cruise around there and suck dick. Mark told me that he gets his dick sucked there when he's horny and his girl won't put out. He says a couple of other guys from the basketball team do it too. If they can't get pussy, they let some guy swing on it. Whaddya think of that?"

"Fuck, I don't know," I said, pausing for a minute to think. The main thing I cared about was that I had now discovered a place nearby where I could meet other guys. No more taking that long trip to Chicago once in a blue moon just to get my rocks off. It seemed too good to be true. And as we stood there in the dark, I started realizing that this might also be a golden opportunity. Joey was horny and so was I. He was the one who had brought up the revelation of cocksuckers in the dark, not me. For once, I got up the nerve to push the odds a little. "I'll tell you, Joey," I whispered, gripping the front of my pants with one hand, "I am horny as can be, and I'd love to get my rocks off."

"Naaah," said Joey, giving me a push and laughing. "You'd do it? You'd let some guy blow you?" But the way he said it, it was like he wanted me to say yes. He'd brought it up. He wanted me to help it along. That way, we were each just going along with the other.

"Hey, man, you said Mark and those other guys got their rocks off that way. Did they say it was any good?"

"Ha! Mark told me that one time it was like the guy blowing him was using a vacuum cleaner."

"Cool," I said, looking at him, and I noticed his hand over his crotch. For a minute there I almost fell to my knees and begged for it, but I knew that would be a disaster. If there was any chance to seduce him, I'd have sensed it. And in a small town, you don't take wild chances just for the hell of it.

Finally, I took the initiative. There was no way I could just go home after getting so worked up. I at least had to see what was down there. "Tell you what, Joey," I said. "I'll walk down there and take a look. It's dark and it'll be easy to sneak up." Taking a sip of my beer, I started down the steep incline to the wooded area below.

Joey paused for a moment, then I heard his footsteps behind me. To the tune of Frank Sinatra's "Strangers in the Night," he started crooning softly, "Blowjobs in the dark...," We both laughed.

As we got to the bottom of the incline, we both shut up and started listening. There was some noise in the trees and bushes ahead of us, but it was hard to tell the exact direction. Joey stood close beside me, and I felt the heat of his big, gawky, horny body there in the dark. More than ever, I wanted my hand to travel those few inches to his crotch. But I knew that wasn't in the cards. With a determination that was really frustration, I walked ahead of him, moving toward some rustling sounds in the bushes about twenty yards away.

First I spotted four guys behind a tall tree, and I stopped before they noticed me. What I saw was pretty clear. One guy in a football jersey was leaning against the tree while a man kneeling in front of him was sucking away at the hard dick sticking through the college kid's fly. I wanted to get a close look at that dick, but I held back. The other two guys there were young and nice looking, but what surprised me was that they were making out! That was something I didn't expect, and I didn't want Joey to see them. Somehow I knew that would turn him off to the idea of our little stroll down Queer Boulevard. It didn't turn me off though! I wished I was there alone so I could walk right over and join those guys.

Joey's footsteps behind me made me turn away from the two couples under the tree and head in another direction. I wanted to try to lead Joey to some kind of scene that he might get into, or maybe I was still hoping he'd pull his rod out and start jacking off. Anyway, he followed me, and in a few minutes I spotted some more strangers in the night.

"Look," Joey said, catching up to me, "there's five guys standing over there against those rocks. You recognize any of them?"

I didn't. But in the moonlight I could see five guys in their twenties and thirties, standing in a row against some large rocks. They weren't talking or paying any attention to each other. It was like they were waiting for something to happen. I decided to do something brave.

"Joey, I'm going over there," I whispered. "I wanna see what happens."

He didn't answer, but I went on ahead and walked right up to the five guys. I was a little scared, but something about the beautiful queerness of the situation kept my dick hard and pressing against my jeans. I stopped in front of the guys—I didn't know any of them—and took a swig of my tall-boy beer to hide my nervousness. I was definitely younger than any of them, and I knew that my long, tangled hair and cute face made me look like Grade-A chicken. Sure enough, the standoff didn't last more than a few seconds. A guy in his thirties reached out and touched the front of my jeans. The first thing he felt was my big, hard dick.

Dropping like a rock, the guy hit the wet mossy ground on both knees and started unzipping me. It turned me on even more that he didn't care that the other guys were crowding around to watch. And when he pulled out my big fat cock, he was like a kid on Christmas Eve.

Hot lips on my hard plunger were just what I needed after a long night of frustration. I had met a much more talented cocksucker on one of my trips to Chicago, but this guy was doing a good, workmanlike job. My dick is a bit more than eight inches long, but the best thing about it is how thick it gets—and this guy on his knees in front of me was in pig heaven. The other guys crowded around and ran their hands over me, or tried to cop a feel of my dick, at least the base of it which the one blowing me couldn't reach with his lips. Meanwhile, I could feel Joey's eyes boring a hole in my back. It was fine getting a nice suck-job, but I was still hoping that Joey would get hot enough to come out of his hiding place and pull out his own dick, or even just watch from up close.

I heard footsteps behind me and prayed that it was him, not just some other cruiser coming to gawk at the action. I looked over my left shoulder and there was Joey, standing just a foot away, watching the show with that lewd grin of his. Two of the cock worshippers made a few tentative steps toward him. Then one made a feel for Joey's basket and submissively got down on his knees.

That was the moment of truth. I was afraid Joey would sock the groper. I kept taking sideways glances, and I could see Joey hesitate, and then make up his mind.

Hooking a thumb into his loose cotton pants, Joey yanked them and his white shorts down to expose his soft cock and balls. Before I could get a better look, that regular-sized pale cock was out of sight, swallowed up by the lucky guy down in front. Oh, man, what I would have given to switch places with that brave out-of-the-closet guy. Of course, he was brave because he was anonymous and probably lived ten or twenty miles away.

My cock throbbed and jumped at the excitement in front of me and in back of me. Every time I turned to take a peek, Joey would just be standing perfectly still with his legs spread, one hand holding his pants down while he held his beer can in the other and took sips. He avoided looking at me, at least when I turned around. I think he was probably digging me getting head right in front of him. Knowing him, I'm sure he liked the rudeness and obsceneness of it all as much as the sensation of a good blowjob.

What's more, he really *was* getting a good blowjob. My guy was doing a so-so job, swallowing about half my thick meat, running his lips along it, and reaching into my open zipper to tickle my balls. Once he pulled off to catch his breath and someone else knelt down to get in a few quick, hot sucks. But Joey was getting the Hoover Special. The cocksucker I envied was motoring away on Joey's cock—and it was really hard after a few minutes of servicing. Although I couldn't see much, I got a good look at it once or twice when the guy pulled back or when Joey's boner got free for a second.

At one point, Joey bent to put his beer down on the ground, then gave his loose pants and shorts a yank down with both hands, exposing his whole cock and his furry balls. If I ever gave myself away, it was in that moment, because I stared hungrily at that cock, before the kneeling guy could go back to servicing it. It was a pretty six inches—no more—but perfectly straight—how appropriate!—and hard as nails. A real pussy-jabber, but now it was jabbing male throat! My own cock suddenly pulsed and swelled all the more, and the guy sucking it made an ecstatic moaning noise. My balls tingled and tightened, and I shot a big load into that hungry, gulping mouth.

As the guy on the ground milked me dry, I turned to watch Joey arching his back. Whatever inhibitions he might have had, Joey had lucked into a fantastic, highspeed blowjob, and nothing could stop him from coming. I watched as he suddenly reached forward and grabbed the guy's hair to yank his head down while he jammed his hips forward. He was coming buckets! I could tell because he kept pumping his hips, and even the expert cocksucker was gagging.

Only when Joey was done did I put my own softening cock away. We left the small crowd of admirers and climbed the grassy slope toward the car.

Later on, Joey would never want to talk about what happened again. But as we walked away from the lovers' lane orgy, he slapped me on the back and said, "Outrageous! We got blown side by side!"

Kerouac at the Everard

Many years after its heyday and shortly before it closed in the mid-eighties, I finally got to see the Everard Baths at 28 West Twenty-eighth Street in Manhattan. Although I'd heard that all kinds of famous people had been there over the decades, including Jack Kerouac, it wasn't history that drew me to the gloomy old building over on the West Side. It was simply the fact that the big, clean, modern bathhouses downtown had closed.

If you want nostalgia, I can only get misty-eyed about the place I loved, and that was the Club Baths on First Avenue between First and Second Streets. Clean rooms on five floors, a lower level with white marble walls and mirrors where you could find your fantasy in the double steam room or community shower or the large whirlpool or dry sauna. Upstairs there was a luxurious television lounge, tropical plants, and an indoor waterfall and garden under a greenhouse roof. And that led to a large, dark orgy room, and a downstairs porn-flick area. Not far away was the St. Marks Baths, more of a barracks-type layout, but with a luxurious lower floor that had a great big steam room, swimming pool, sauna, and hot tub.

What's more, the downtown places had the hot boys, from the flocks of hunky Hispanics at the Club to the rock-solid gym bodies you'd find at the St. Marks.

And so I can't pretend that the Everard of the late seventies and early eighties could compare to the bathhouses that were popular among the hip, young, and beautiful. But on the other hand, it didn't take too much imagination to see it the way it must have been in the fifties when Kerouac went there on a lark.

The night I checked it out, I was impressed by the size of the building from the outside, since it was as big as the modern baths downtown. But right away I was put off by the institutional look of the place. A wide, timeworn staircase led up to the main floor, and a line of guys waited to check in. Some of these men were shabbily dressed and fumbling with bags that seemed to hold all of their belongings. This was a long way from the sleek atmosphere of bathhouses I'd seen from coast to coast.

Adding to the men's-shelter decor was a wire cage window at the check-in entrance. The crabby old clerk and the beat-up guys dragging around mops were also a far cry from the cute boys you expect to see working at most baths. But I didn't want to travel all the way home without giving the place a chance, and I noticed a few other young guys on line—downtown types who looked just as out of place and curious as I did.

There were no rooms available, so I got one of those "walk-in" rooms, which is really a glorified broom closet. Once I got my threadbare towel and walked into the place, my dick shrank up a little more. Instead of track lighting or glass chandeliers, I saw flickering fluorescent lights and naked bulbs hanging on overhead wires. But when I got undressed in my walk-in, I started to loosen up a little bit. In the first place, I knew that a dark-haired young guy had checked in just before me and was getting undressed a few doors away. That alone made my nine-incher spring out to full length before I could get my towel wrapped around me. With any luck, I figured I'd snag that guy somewhere in the building, and the thought of it was hot. He had plain good looks and he was a bit shorter than me, but nicely proportioned I could tell.

I also noticed some of the graffiti on the plywood walls around me. SUCKED ALEX HERE SIX TIMES, BIG HARD BLACK DICK. Another read, FUCK YOU FAGGOTS! Followed by the answer, THAT'S THE IDEA, SWEETIE, and another, NOT TOO QUICK, IS HE? A really faded message promised, GROOVY HEAD FOR IN-SHAPE GUYS, TUESDAY NIGHTS IN SAUNA ROOM. And a brand-new one prophesied the obvious: SEX POLICE WILL CLOSE THIS PLACE SOON.

The hell with the past and future, I thought I was hoping to hear the other guy's door open so I could time my own exit from the room, but the place was noisy and I slowly realized I'd waited too long. With my towel folded to half its width and tied tightly around me, I knew my half-hard dick was well on display against the thin material. Wishing myself luck, I emerged from the tiny room and started walking the dank corridors of the Everard.

A stairway on the left side of the building led to the upper floors and the rooms. Except for the run-down condition of the place, that part of the Everard seemed familiar. There were several floors of rooms with narrow corridors. The doors were locked, or kept slightly ajar, or in some cases wide open.

On the third floor I got to see some action. Actually, I practically had to push my way through a crowd to see. At the end of a corridor there were seven or eight men looking into a room which had its door half-open. I didn't want to join the pack of voyeurs, but the air of sex-fever told me that it was worth a look.

"No, it's too big," a raspy voice pleaded in a low whine. That got my attention. I angled my way past a few old gaffers and what I saw was intriguing. It seemed that a distinguished gray-haired man in his fifties had lured a hunky young brute into his room— probably with the usual offer of a blowjob—and had gotten more than he could handle! The stocky, unshaven guy in his thirties had easily flipped the older man onto his stomach and was already stuffing his horse dick into his host's pale, quivering butt. Since the older guy was slim and not bad looking, this made for a pretty good show.

"Take that big dick," the rough stud growled, and he slammed home about half of his crowbar-hard dick. The older guy gasped and his legs kicked up from the spearing he was getting, but it was plain that he was getting what he really wanted. What he didn't want was an audience. As the muscle-stud started to move his piston hips in a powerful fuck motion, the gray-haired guy reached for the door, to try to swing it closed. But the relentless fucker kicked out a foot to swing the door open even more. He was getting off on having witnesses to his all out ass assault.

This was not the kind of scene I'd ever experienced at the pretty-boy bars or the downtown after-hours clubs. It was rough and rude and—and my own dick was standing up at attention!

What followed was predictable. As the big guy fucked harder

and faster, the skewered senior citizen went limp as a rag doll, surrendering his ass and himself to the pleasure-pounding he was getting.

At first I resisted when I felt a hand, then a mouth, on my protruding prick. But then I gave in to the service offered. I didn't even look at whose head was working between the towel I held open around my waist—I knew well enough there weren't any Prince Charmings in the crowd that I stood with. Still, it was hot to watch such a rough fuck in progress while a cock-hungry mouth slobbered over my own stiff rod.

Finally the big muscular guy started a steady slam-fuck motion that meant he was getting close. With his powerful hands he lifted the older man's slim, pink butt off the mattress and held it in position to take every inch of his demanding dick. The old guy was moaning and blubbering helplessly, but he took his medicine like a pro. After all, I figured, this was not his first time around the block, or at the Everard.

Only when the younger man's fuck thrusts went out of control did I notice the ring of a clear-latex rubber which was encircling his shaft more than an inch up from the base. It was still the early years of safe fucking, and it left a good impression on me. The guy must have filled the tip of that rubber because he kept pounding away for a couple of minutes before he finally let up. Then he gently detached his still-hard dick from the blushing butt. He lowered the moaning man's exhausted body to the mattress and stood over him like the sex master he was. That was my cue to back away from the frantic cock-eater who was kneeling in front of me, and, wrapping my towel back in place, I strode down the corridor and all the way back down the dank stairway to the first floor.

A badly faded sign directed the way to the lower level with the pool, sauna, and steam room. That's usually my favorite part of any bathhouse and, even though I was disappointed by what I found, it was true at the Everard too.

The basement floor had a good-sized swimming pool, but let us say it did not look inviting. Although I was three decades away from the great polio scare of the fifties, there was nothing that could make me dive into those murky waters.

Around the pool there were old tacky yellow plastic chairs. The men sitting there, like the place, had seen better days. Likewise, the radio tunes bouncing off the old tile walls of the cavernous bathing area weren't the latest dance numbers but rather old fart Frank Sinatra scoobie-doobie-doo stuff.

A couple of thirty-something guys like myself came out of the small shower room and sat beside the pool while they dried themselves. "Join us for a smoke," one of them said, and I did. Although the two guys—lovers, I think—left ten minutes later, they did put me in a different frame of mind.

Ignoring the plastic chairs, the pathetic music, and the run-down condition of the place, I began to see the large room as it once was. Huge columns stretched all the way up to the high ceiling; the sense of space and luxury was still there.

I took a quick shower in the side room and imagined how much cruising and fooling around went on under those four shower heads over the years. Instead of drying myself, I left my towel on one of the wall hooks in the big room and walked over to the steam bath.

Opening the glass door to the steam room, I was hit by thick clouds of vapor. The moist heat seemed clean and warm enough, and I stepped inside and shut the door behind me. The size of the room was impressive. I made my way around the big oval space, unable to see much in the heavy mist. There were tiled seating levels along the walls, and just as I found a good spot in an alcove, the door opened.

It was hard to see, but I recognized the slim form of a Chinese guy in his late twenties, someone who had been cruising me when I sat by the pool. As he made his way around the room, trying to find me in the dark and steam, I started pulling on my cock.

By the time he found me, I was sitting back against the tile wall, my legs spread and my fat hard-on pointing to the ceiling. He hesitated, then tentatively reached out and found my offering. Once his fingers wrapped around my hard shaft and explored the length and thickness of it, he dropped to his knees and got to work.

I rubbed his thin shoulders with my hands, encouraging him to bring me off. His mouth got a vacuum hold on my cock, and he sucked it greedily while he fondled my balls. His lips got every inch of my rod, from the sensitive head all the way to the prongy base. This guy must have been aching for cockmeat all night. Everyone's had nights like that—and that kind of horniness usually leads to hot sex when it finally happens.

When I felt myself getting close to shooting, I stood up in the steamy heat and wrapped my hands around the Chinese guy's head, holding him tightly as I started ram-fucking his throat. Just as I figured, this only turned him on more. He hoovered my hard-on and beat his own cock at lightning speed, and within seconds I reached the point of no return. It was great to stand tall and blast my load against the tonsils of such a fantastic cocksucker. He moaned as hot bolts of come filled his mouth, and he whipped his own cock until he shot his smoldering cream onto the wet tile floor. My arms dangled at my sides as he milked my cock with his satisfied lips. Then he jumped up and made for the door and the showers, leaving me to slump back into my seat in the steam room.

I can take the steam for longer than most people, and I sat there in a kind of blissful haze for a while. Then I started to daydream a little, especially about the story I'd heard about Jack Kerouac's one night at the Everard.

A young Allen Ginsberg and other gay friends convinced Kerouac to come along with them to the baths one night, back in the fifties. Ginsberg in those days was good at getting the pants off his straight writer friends, like Kerouac and Neal Cassady. Anyway, one night he got Jack away from his girlfriends and his hang-ups, and there they all were—walking around at the Everard in towels.

When I'd first heard the story, it was just a famous underground rumor. But in recent years it's been confirmed in the biography *Ginsberg,* by Barry Miles. It seems that before the night was over, Kerouac let down his guard—and his towel! And, while his friends watched, he got a hot blowjob from a whole group of French sailors who knelt and worshipped at his feet. "I think he just dug the idea of a bunch of French sailors," Ginsberg told his biographer.

Now, as I relaxed in the steam in my postorgasmic bliss, I tried to conjure up the scene. I know what Kerouac's body was like— short and compact and perfectly proportioned. And his face was the all-American handsome type, with the kind of medium butch cut of the fifties. His cock I imagined would be as straight as a two-inch-wide length of pipe, and it would get unusually stiff and hard and stay that way until long after he came.

I tried to imagine where in the Everard the blowjob scene happened...and I couldn't imagine any more likely spot than right there in the steam room. After all, it was big enough for a crowd—which no cubicle would hold—but it was still kind of private, away from the nettlesome nellies and the gawking gaffers who would make Jack uncomfortable.

I opened my eyes and looked across the steamy expanse of the Turkish bath. Directly across from me was a wide shelf which would have been a perfect spot for Jack to sit and spread his beefy thighs.

I imagined the scene: Young Ginsberg and other friends are sitting along the same shelf close to him. A whole bevy of young French sailors, jabbering in their native language, come in through the door. Despite their French arrogance, the five cute young sailors, ranging in age from nineteen to twenty-five, are immediately turned on by the hot body and butch stance of Kerouac. They talk more quietly among themselves but move closer to where the Americans are sitting in the steamy room.

For his part, Jack is enjoying all the attention and is turned on by the sound of the French patter. To his surprise, he feels his cock hardening, and then he sees that the French boys have become transfixed, looking at his growing dick. That makes his meat stand straight up—and the first Frenchie hits the pavement, kneading between Jack's legs and bending down to kiss his balls.

None of Jack's girlfriends has ever paid attention to his sensitive balls, and he spreads his legs wider as the guy licks and kisses away. Suddenly, all five of the French sailors are kneeling and crouching before him. A mouth engulfs his stiff cock and starts sucking away. Hands massage his thighs, his solid torso.

Just before he gives in completely, Jack thinks of jumping up and running out, of getting his clothes and going directly to his latest girlfriend's house. But how many drinks and how much talk would it take before he got her in bed? And what would she do then, besides make like a rag doll and wait for him to fuck her? Jack sighs and relaxes, giving in to the sucking mouths that fight for his cock and pleasure his balls, and the massaging hands that rub him all over.

Leaning back against the tile wall, he arcs his hips forward so that his cock stands forward like an iron bar, towering over the French boys who worship his dick and balls and body like nobody ever has. When one of the cocksuckers seems much better at eating dick than the others, Jack grabs him by the hair and holds him in place, pulling the kid down over his demanding rod, back and forth until his balls tighten up against his body. Then Jack's whole physique tenses, his hips slam forward, and he shoots his wad as he holds the guy's head in place; shooting his seed all the way down the French boy's gullet.

Crashing stars, flashes of light, and magic crystal colors blind his eyes, and then he feels the currents of electricity coursing up and down his limbs, slowing and fading. And then he realizes he's standing, still holding the kneeling French guy, still plugging his face with his hard cock, while the others are running their hands up and down his legs and torso.

Exhausted and totally spent, Jack falls back onto the slippery tiled shelf and leans against the wall. The French sailors crowd again, still taking turns sucking his throbbing cock. "Damn," says one of Allen's friends, "he fucks the way he writes."

The steam room door opened and I looked up. Somebody was

100

stepping into the room. I blinked and looked back to the wide shelf across from me. The vision of Kerouac and the French sailors was gone. Gone but not forgotten.

I looked up at the guy approaching me in the darkened steam room. Clouds of fresh vapor made it hard to see, and then I realized it was the dark-haired young guy I'd seen when I first checked in. He stood right in front of me, still wearing his towel. I reached underneath it and felt a plump set of balls and a nice cock that was getting stiff to my touch.

At the same time, the wiry young stud was reaching down to handle my cock, which had gotten hard again during my fantasy about Kerouac. I stood up and we kept playing with each other, both wanting to suck the other's cock.

Finally I led the guy across the slippery floor, to the other side of the room where the wide shelf gave us a place to stretch out. And that's what we did, sixty-nining in that same spot where I imagined the hot scene had taken place three decades earlier.

Pretty soon, as the firm young cock ploughed away at my face, and I started to bury my own cock in the other guy's throat, I forgot all about the past and enjoyed the present

Still, sometimes it's hard to tell the difference between then and now.

The Anvil

The Anvil was one of the hottest and most notorious after-hours clubs in the wild days of the seventies and eighties. No pun intended, but it was in the "meat packing" district of New York, right there on the grimy back streets where sides of beef got warehoused in the day—and slabs of meat got handled at night.

The upstairs at the Anvil was a scene worthy of the Roman Circus. If you arrived at the appropriate time, after all the regular bars had closed, you'd find the place packed, with naked young studs dancing on the bar tops and using ropes suspended from the ceiling to swing from one bar to the other and up onto the stage. The stage, in the center of the upstairs level, provided some wild entertainment as the hour grew late—everything from sex acts to fire-eaters.

Some people might remember that the disco group The Village People was inspired by the Anvil, and a couple of regular dancers from the club became members of that successful pop band. My favorite was the hot young man who dressed as an Indian. For years he was a regular at the Gay Pride Parade and a celebrity at the Anvil. It was hilarious that straight America made The Village People big stars for a couple of years. The U.S. Navy nearly used the song "In the Navy" for a recruitment campaign—until someone actually listened to the words, and then all of the dimwitted public realized that this band was as gay as a barber pole.

There was also a back room upstairs—beyond the bars, the stage, and the dance floor. On a crowded night, it took a lot of trouble to get there. But if you made it, your reward would be some action of your choice in a darkened room, lit only by a small porn video screen. That was okay, but I preferred the downstairs.

Downstairs at the Anvil was a long horizontal space that was the gone-to-hell opposite of the clean cut, all American basement recreation room. Once you got down the narrow staircase, the bar to your left looked normal enough. But then, on either side of that bar, you would notice cavelike openings in the cellar wall. Inside the openings was a long, narrow, pitch-dark backroom which was cramped and creepy but ideal for private blowjobs. Not much room there for anything else.

In the center of the downstairs floor was a large video screen which showed red-hot porn on both sides—I don't think I've seen a double screen like that since. People could watch porn-action from their places at the bar, or from the far side of the room, where there was a wooden, corral-like enclosure for dancing, although the Anvil's downstairs was too cruisy and sex charged for much dancing.

There was more. Behind the video screens and the small dance area were some openings in the long back wall. These led to a large back room, a dark, oddly shaped space where most of the action at the Anvil went on. It was a great place to fool around, or just to watch. After a few drinks and watching some hot porn and maybe checking out a few sexy guys in the crowd—well, that backroom really came in handy.

Backroom sex is really interesting. Just as it was with the baths in the good old days, backroom action can bring out the best in guys—or the worst, depending on how you see it. The dynamics can get wild when there's no reason to pretend. I remember one time when a pudgy, sort of pretty young guy followed me into the backroom behind the video screen. He was dressed too daintily for the Anvil, and I don't know what he was doing there. Slumming, I guess. He was wearing expensive slacks, good shoes, and a bright red silk dress shirt. Fuck, everyone else was in denim or leather.

Anyway, fancy pants kept following me back and forth as I scouted out the action in the backroom. I wasn't interested in him, but I hate to say no to people when they're really interested in me. After all, I hate it when someone gives me the cold shoulder. So I decided to give the young fashion plate the downtown dick he wanted—but only if he did it *my* way.

My way was to stand with my back to the wall, just inside the cave-like opening on the left side of the dark playroom. That way I could look out and see the video screen, which at that moment was showing a hot flick about a blond and a Puerto Rican. The guys out in the main room, at least the ones by the bar, could see into the half-dark space where I was standing. The uptown preppie had come to the Anvil to ogle the denim and leather set and get turned on—so it was only fair that he should become part of the show.

He hesitated at first. Prim and proper, he timidly stood next to me and brushed a small white hand against my bulging basket.

When he saw that I didn't mind, he gave it a squeeze and got a good feel of my ample, half-hard cock. Then I popped the button of my jeans. He could have it, but he had to take it right there. According to unspoken backroom rules, that was my right. Besides, I knew that once he got into it, it would turn him on twice as much to blow his cover as well as *me*.

The soft-skinned young man slid a hand down the front of my open jeans. No underwear, so he immediately had a handful of hot cock. And his dainty little fingers felt good—my thick prong stiffened up and stood out from my open zipper. Unable to hesitate any more, the well-dressed guy forgot his priggish pride and did the old universal dive for dick. He knelt before me, his expensive slacks on the grungy cellar floor, and wrapped his lips around the flesh tube of his fantasies. This drew a crowd—more than it would have in the darkened recesses of the back room.

Several people from the hidden, darkened area moved up closer to get a better look at the hot blowjob-in-progress. At the same time, some guys in the bar area were now dividing their attention between the sexy porn video and the live action provided by me and my admirer.

To give the preppie his due, he could suck cock! His thick, juicy lips were playing a nice tune on my love-tube. Maybe he couldn't swallow the whole length of my hard dick, but he was getting three-quarters of the way down the shaft, banging the back of his throat against my fat dickhead, then sliding his lips lovingly backwards, only to plunge forward again. He was so good that I made a mental note never to reject people on first impression; they might just surprise you.

At one point—you could see it in his startled eyes—my

cultured cocksucker remembered where he was. He was on the dirty floor of a notorious bar with a mouthful of dick and a fairly good-sized audience. He backed off my rod and made a move to get up and retreat. My tingling balls and my instincts told me what to do. I brought my hands up on his silk shirt and gave his shoulders a shove back down. Of course I wouldn't stop him if he really wanted to get up, but I knew the extra thrill of being treated rough would drive him over the edge. Was I ever right!

The preppie went back to work with renewed gusto, sucking like a vacuum on high speed. I knew my pulsing prong couldn't take such a sweet suck-job for long. I arched my hips forward and got ready to come. At the same time, he opened his designer slacks and pulled out his dainty white dick, which he proceeded to wank like crazy. We were both at that high point where we didn't care about our audience, just about coming.

His eyes looked like headlamps as he got the first blast of my hot load. But he stayed right with it, swallowing and sucking without missing a beat. Finally, I had to make him slow down on my sensitive, satisfied dick. I held his head steady as his lips massaged just the end of my still-hard cock. Then his speedy jerk-off skills brought him off, and he let out a loud moan that surprised even me—and got the attention of just about everyone within earshot. His lips slid forward all the way to the base of my rod for the first time. Totally satisfied, he hung there for a long moment, like a side of beef on a hook. Then he scrambled to his feet, brushed off his slacks and rushed across the main room and up the stairs.

Of course, I know how sweet it is when someone hot yanks your chain—so to speak. Another time, on a weekday night at the Anvil, I found the downstairs nearly deserted. I had a drink, watched a video, and thought about heading home. But I figured maybe it would be worth ducking into the dark, hidden areas in search of a quickie.

The small backroom, the one behind the bar, was totally empty. I figured the same might be true of the larger play area, the one behind the video screen. But when I went inside, I heard noises from the darkest part of the interior.

Slowly I inched my way along in the dark, running my hand along the uneven wall until my eyes adjusted. Then I saw a couple of guys in a corner, groping and kissing each other. Nothing too interesting. I started to head back through the opening in the wall when suddenly a tall figure blocked my way.

There was just enough light to see that the young man was okay looking, not beautiful, and that his tall, wiry body was solidly muscled under his denim jeans, shirt, and jacket. Without pausing, he reached for the front of my pants and started massaging my meat. I opened up and unzipped for him, and he began to stroke my stiffening cock with a large hand. I waited for a blowjob, but then I realized he was waiting for one too! Seeing his big hard-on sticking out of his jeans, I impulsively took hold of it.

What a salami. My hard-on is big and fat, but his was bigger and fatter. I forgot about my own dick for a minute as I tried to wrap my fingers around the thick base of his rod. But I couldn't! What a tree trunk—and it just got bigger and stiffer while I massaged it

No question, this young hunk wanted a taste of my dick. But he was waiting until I paid first tribute to his monster cock. We stood there in the dark, stroking each other from a few inches away in a kind of standoff. Finally I decided: The hell with this—he wins. After all, he had the bigger artillery. I got down in the dark and gave willing lip service to that massive cockmeat. It was just a great big dick that was fun to suck. I squirmed a hand into his open pants to take hold of his balls, which were about average size. Though nobody could take too much of such an overgrown gourd, I gave it the kind of sucking it deserved, and I would have been content to suck him off right away. But he put his hands under my armpits to lift me up. He wanted a slab of beef too. And on those lonely weeknights when the bars are near empty, a guy can get really hot for cock. So we took turns for a while, standing and kneeling, sucking each other for long minutes in the dark before returning the favor. I finally came in his hot mouth while he shot in his own hand, but it would've been just as good the other way too.

Since we're not likely to see a place like the Anvil again, it's worth remembering all these things. In fact, I almost forgot to mention the hottest thing I ever saw there. To make things more interesting, it happened to be a night when I brought a curious straight friend along. He wasn't curious to see a gay bar or about the club's wild reputation. He was anxious to hear the music, because it was New Wave Night at the Anvil, and the DJ was really fantastic. So, the original plan was to stay upstairs, have a few drinks, and listen to the music.

My straight pal enjoyed the music and the wild atmosphere. Soon, another kind of curiosity hit him. "Do guys really have sex here?" he asked. He knew the answer to that. What he was really saying was: Show me.

I brought him downstairs and into the back room. He stood close to me—afraid of getting groped, I guess. Well, luck was with us. Right inside the opening of the big play area, where there was just enough light to see, two hot young guys were fucking dog style like there was no tomorrow.

Both had their pants down to their ankles, and one was bent all the way forward while his buddy buttfucked him. The fucker held his pal firmly by the hips and just piston-fucked him. It was wild, that big hard dick slamming in and out of a hot young butt, their flesh slapping, the crowd around them gasping at the sight, and some guys stroking their dicks.

Nobody can fuck like that all the time, and few ever hit such a peak of frenzy. I could hardly take my eyes off the two smoldering-hot, exhibitionist fuckers. But I did manage to steal a glance at my straight pal who was standing close beside me, his hands protectively folded in front of his crotch. Well, let me tell you, his mouth was open, and his eyes were almost bulging out. Differences in sexuality begin and end at a certain point—all he knew was that he'd never seen the like! And, believe it or not, neither had I.

The guy getting fucked twisted and turned as he got drilled. He didn't know what to do with his arms—they swung in front of him like those of a rag doll. Then he covered his face. Then he pinched his own nipples.

The guy doing the fucking was relentless. He was like a machine, holding the other's slim hips in a viselike grip while pounding harder and harder, faster and faster. I know that it's easier to fuck standing up, because you don't use up much of your strength holding yourself over the person you're fucking. But this guy in the back room was really making the most of that advantage.

When he came, he drove so fast and furious into his buddy's battered ass, you could hardly believe it. He came buckets, you could tell. Then he continued to spear that well-fucked ass, nice and slow, while he reached around and whacked off his friend's hard dick. Finally they pulled apart, their pants still down, and started to move away. I reached out and grabbed the hot fucker's still-hard dick. If it wasn't all gooed up, I might have gone down on it, right in front of my shocked friend. His dick was still hard as a rock and pulsing. He reached to pull up his pants, then started to walk away from me—but not before taking a squeeze of the front of my jeans. Needless to say, I was sporting my own back-room boner.

Outside the bar, as we waved for a taxi in the bright light of dawn, my poor straight friend was still shaking his head, still seeing that hot sight before his shocked eyes. "That," he said, "was just fucking unbelievable!" And that's just one of the reasons I will never forget the Anvil.

Fire Island Threesome

Tommy and I had arrived at Fire Island an hour before I spotted Billy. I knew right away that Billy would make the holiday weekend more wild than relaxing.

Tommy was twenty-three and I was thirty and the world seemed all ours that summer. When our ferry had arrived at the Cherry Grove docks, it was romantic and exciting to see the bright-colored wooden buildings and the rainbow flags and banners flying.

While Tommy unpacked in our little room, I got into a T-shirt and bathing suit. My dark hair was long that summer. At six feet, with a regular build, my best feature had always been my well-hung equipment. But my younger lover had me beat there. Blond Tommy was just as tall as me—though with a more full build—but his dick was simply humongous. Once, one of my straight friends, seeing Tommy undressed, had blurted out, "Tommy, you have an enormous dick!" It was just a fact. We had long ago nicknamed his fat eleven-incher "Beastie."

111

Tommy was still playing house when I stepped outside and walked the length of the famous Beach Hotel. I could tell by the layout and the number of hot guys that it would be a very cruisy weekend. I walked to the front of the hotel and saw a group of young guys standing in front of the nearby bar, the Monster. One of them was Billy.

Billy had the hottest, most mouth-watering body I'd ever seen. The healthy teeth in his big-lipped smile sort of went this way and that, but even so his face was cute. Back in the city, he sometimes tricked with Tommy. I didn't mind; Tommy and I allowed each other some freedom. But in this case, I was jealous. I wanted Billy too.

Billy's dick was a beaut, according to Tommy. "It curves up and gets really hard," he had told me, "but it's nice and velvety and pretty."

I could imagine. All you had to do was look at Billy's skin, that healthy translucent color, and you knew his body was delicious, from his thick pouty lips down to the root of his cock.

He knew I liked him. He'd made it with Tommy three or four times, probably more. Once he nearly got it on with me, but we got interrupted. He really dug Tommy, but he liked me well enough. When I saw that he was on Fire Island for the weekend, it got my horny hopes racing.

I walked over the patch of grassy path leading to the Monster and went up to Billy.

"Hey, Junior!" he called. "You and Tommy out here for the weekend? Far out!" The cute guys he'd been talking to turned to check me out, but my eyes were only on Billy.

He was wearing low sneakers with no socks, white shorts with no underwear—you could tell—and an aqua-colored tank top that revealed his flat, muscular belly. His whole body was a golden bronze color. Billy never worked, but it was obvious he'd been a "guest" on the island a lot that summer.

Billy's friends were ignoring me once they saw I was only a pal of his. They were common trade. Billy was also trade, but with his friends he was just a sweet horny kid from Long Island.

I told him that Tommy and I were staying at the Beach Hotel and gave him our room number.

"Well, I gotta hang out with some guys who have a house at the other side of the Grove," Billy said. "Some guys who are sorta putting me up. But why don't you two meet me at the bar when I'm free, about closing time tonight?" Then he awkwardly leaned forward to give me a full kiss with those bedroom lips of his. A minute later he was off with the others.

I bought two huge tropical drinks in plastic cups and went back to the room to give Tommy the good news.

That night, the Monster was packed to overflowing, and you could hear the disco music blaring from far away. Tommy and I got along with everybody, but we didn't really fit in with the disco crowd. We were drinking beer outside the bar when Billy came along on the wooden walkway. He was wearing white slacks and a long-sleeved white cotton shirt, which showed off his tan even more.

We bought more beer and went down to the beach on the ocean side. There was a half-moon, and far out on the water you could see the lights of a few fishing boats. We walked along in the sand, listening to the surf crashing along the shore.

I guess Tommy and I had an understanding about one thing.

113

We wanted to break the ice between Billy and me. If we could do that, then maybe we'd warm up to a really hot threesome later in the weekend. After more than an hour of walking around and talking, we put our plan into action.

We were lying on the beach in a kind of triangle. It was no accident that I was only inches away from Billy's basket His sexy package of cock and balls was clearly outlined in the white cotton slacks. We'd stopped talking, and I just stared at that juicy basket, and finally I dived for it.

"Wha...Junior...wait," Billy started to sputter, but Tommy moved in like military air power protecting the infantry. He planted a big kiss on Billy's mouth and put his arms around him.

They were making out big time while I chewed Billy's beef through his thin slacks. Then I opened his belt, undid the pants, and pulled his prize out from a pair of sexy bikini briefs.

Even half-hard, his cock was beautiful. Already I could see how thick it was at the base and how pretty the shaft and rosy head were. It was as smooth as silk to the touch. Even though he was about Tommy's age, Billy's balls were as pink as baby skin. His pubic hair was a dark blond color. Right away I was getting a real close look as I wrapped my lips around his cock.

His boy-banana had a clean, fresh taste and scent. It stayed sort of rubbery for a minute, then started lengthening and thickening in my mouth. It was so hot to have that lusty dick come to life between my lips. It curved and stiffened and finally hooked into a long, hard arc pointing up to the moon.

I had my own slacks pulled down as I worked my excited hard-on with my free hand. But suddenly I felt Tommy's hands on my balls and cock, and then I felt his warm lips. I was completely happy with Billy's boner, but I was curious enough to look up. Sure enough, Billy's pouty lips were stretched around Tommy's famous Beastie prong, and Tommy completed the triangle by sucking my hard rod. If anyone could see us out there on the beach, we were giving them some hot show. Think of all that dick! With my thick nine-incher, Billy's eight-inch curver, and Tommy's eleven-inch baloney, that was two feet four inches of solid cock!

We might have all come just like that, but I was too greedy for Billy's tasty treat. Since I couldn't get it all from my sideways position, I broke away from Tommy and got between Billy's legs in the sand. I couldn't see what those other two were doing, and I didn't care. All that mattered was that I was able to deep-throat Billy's hard-hooking prong all the way to the balls. His smooth, hard abdomen was all I could see as he started bucking and thrusting up at me.

Moans came from both of them just as Billy started spraying his load into my mouth and throat. I guess he was taking Tommy's truckload at the same time. I was wild from the taste of the young stud's sweet come, and I shot into the sand as I milked his rod.

We stretched out in the sand for a long time, sort of caressing each other. We all knew how special a good threesome was. Suddenly it was getting brighter, and we realized we'd been on the beach for hours. Lavender shades of dawn were lightening up the sky.

Before heading back, we all stripped and ran into the ocean for a swim. It was great to see their happy laughing faces bobbing in the rough water around me.

It was well past noon when I woke in our room at the Beach Hotel. I could hear disco music and the sounds of the swimming-pool crowd. Next to me on the bed, Tommy was naked and half-awake. It always surprised me how normal his cock looked when it was soft. Billy's bronzed body was stretched across the other bed, a sleeper's hard-on poking through his bikini briefs. It took some willpower, but I didn't wake the sleeping beauty.

We had lunch on the pool terrace—tropical drinks and omelets with sliced fruit. After that, I figured I'd give Billy and Tommy some space. I knew how hot they were for each other. I got a deck chair by the pool and read for about an hour. Then before long Tommy was standing over me with a funny smile on his face.

"Billy says that we should all go inside for a while," he said.

Inside the room, Billy was sitting on one of the beds, wearing just a towel around his waist. I sat next to him, and Tommy sat on the other bed and slipped out of his bathing suit. He looked at us with a grin as he started stroking his cock.

Billy and I talked a little bit, then he leaned over my lap and tugged down my swimsuit. He held my growing cock in his hand, looked up at me, and smiled. Then he went down on it with those fat, juicy lips.

When he stretched out on his stomach on the bed, his towel fell to the floor. I knew he didn't like to get fucked, but I started rubbing his hard melon buns and giving them little spanks. I couldn't get to his cock which was pressed against the mattress under him.

Across the room, naked, with his legs spread and his outrageous cock sticking up like a field cannon, Tommy was burning up from the sight of Billy slow-sucking my salami. I was getting pretty heated up myself, with Billy's warm, spongy lips on my cock, his perfect butt in my hands, and Tommy and Beastie just out of reach.

Ten minutes or so we stayed like that, but Billy was a dedicated cocksucker, not necessarily a good one. I knew he'd never get me off that way. Finally I lifted him up into a sitting position, and his hard handlebar dick sprang into view.

Before you could blink, I was on my knees on the floor and Billy was standing with his milk-and-honey horn in my mouth. Almost as fast, Tommy sprung across the room and got on the floor beneath me. After Billy's slow, teasing suck-job, Tommy's talented lips on my rod sent electric waves up and down my body.

I wanted Billy to come in my mouth at the same time I got off, but my tingling balls couldn't wait any more. Tommy squirmed into a perfect position as my right hand grabbed his head and I started to mouth-fuck him. I held Billy's fuzzy balls in my other hand and just as I started to shoot, I went all the way down on his stiff shaft. I swallowed every bit of his crowbar-hard dick as Tommy kept his mouth sealed around my gushing throbber.

That should have been all for me, and I figured I'd just watch those two get it on, but Tommy had other ideas. He stood up next to Billy, facing me where I still knelt on the floor. Anyone who loves cock would have paid a king's ransom to switch places with me. Side by side, Billy's glistening pretty cock stood up at attention, and Tommy's fat monster meat hung down from its own weight. It didn't matter that I had just come; I'd never seen anything hotter.

Those two were pinching nipples and making out. I stayed right where I was and tried to service both cocks, sucking one for a few minutes, and then going to the other. When I felt Billy's thighs tighten up and press against my chest, I stayed on his juicy beauty while it squirted a nice load. Then I got back on my lover's prize prong. I played with his balls just the way he liked, and within a few minutes I brought him off myself for the first time that weekend.

Arm in arm, Billy and Tommy fell back on one bed while I stretched out on the other. Twenty-four hours earlier, they wouldn't have done that in front of me, but now we were completely relaxed with one another. I liked seeing them together like that; they were both so damned sexy. I only wished I could have seen what happened next.

Between every two rooms there was a hallway with a bathroom and shower. You shared it with your neighbor across the hall.

"Phew," Billy said, bending down to pick up his towel from the floor, "I'm going to take a shower."

As soon as Billy went in the hall leading to the bathroom, Tommy got a funny look in his eyes—as if he were trying to make up his mind. Then he said it.

"I want him to fuck me," he blurted out, then grabbed a towel and rushed after Billy. I hesitated. In fact, I hesitated too long.

First, I was surprised. I didn't think Tommy ever let anyone fuck him besides me. All right, so now I knew. But maybe Tommy didn't want me to see him getting fucked by anyone else. Maybe Billy would feel funny screwing my lover if I was watching. Maybe I'd feel funny. But, what the hell, it *had to* be hot.

I grabbed a towel and rushed out to the hallway. I could hear the shower running, but the bathroom door was locked. They didn't want the guys from the adjoining room to walk in. Even though they were both under the shower, I was about to knock on the door when I realized I was too late.

Wham! Bam! Wham! That sound could only mean one thing. Tommy was getting slammed against the metal shower stall while Billy fucked him silly. So I didn't get to see the action, but I didn't feel completely left out. It was hot just to hear the racket they were making.

Ten minutes later they came back into the room. Tommy had a sheepish grin while Billy looked guilty.

"Well, Billy fucked me good," Tommy said.

"If you don't mind..." Billy added—absurdly, since it was a little late to worry if I minded.

Billy hurried into his clothes. He had to get back across the Grove, to spend some time with his hosts. He knew Tommy and I would be gone after the weekend, and he needed to earn his keep out there on the island.

"I'll find you guys again tonight, late," he said.

After he left, things seemed kind of empty. Tommy and I curled up together and got some sleep. Later, after dinner, it seemed like the night dragged on forever.

By the time we met Billy at the Monster late that night, we were all tired. We got a last-call drink and carried it outdoors. Billy looked hot in his sleeveless T-shirt and white shorts, but his long-lashed eyes were closing.

"What did they do to you over at that house where you're staying?" I asked, giving his basket a little squeeze.

"Oh, you know," he said with that toothy grin, "they just collected the rent."

Yeah. And probably some back rent too, I thought. Billy was one tired puppy. "Tommy and I are going to have to adopt you," I said. "Then we'll always take care of you."

"That would be great," Billy said with a grin and a dreamy look that was more than half-serious.

He put one arm on my shoulder and one arm on Tommy's, and

we walked him back to the room. What happened that night was different than I had planned.

Billy got out of his clothes and fell across the spare bed. As soon as his hot bod hit the mattress, buns up, he was out like a light

"He wouldn't even know if he got buttfucked tonight," I said, only half-joking.

"Naw," Tommy said. "He wouldn't like that. You can fuck me."

That sounded fine to me. But when we stripped and climbed into our bed, it seemed like we were going to poop out too.

"Hah!" Tommy smirked, shaking my sleepy, soft dick. That put me off for a minute, as I leaned back on the comfortable pillows. But little did we know that Tommy had offended the universal god of cock. He needed a lesson about respecting the power of dick.

When I gave my cock the slightest tug, it was like starting up an engine. It jumped. It thickened. It pulsed and stretched and straightened more and more, until it was a thick nine-inch tower with a beautifully ridged dome. Tommy, who was well acquainted with my meat after two years together, stared at it like he'd never seen it before.

"That really looks good," he said. Then he scrunched down to the bottom of the bed, got down between my thighs, and wrapped his lips around my hard throbber.

Tommy could suck. He always could, but usually everybody was too interested in his monster Beastie prong to give him a chance at their dicks. Catch him in a cock-hungry mood, though, and you were in for a treat

He played with my balls and got right to work. His moist lips worked every inch of my stiff rod, from the crown down to the base, his nose touching my pubic curlies. When he was hot for a mouthful of dick, there was no stupid licking and teasing; he just wanted to suck off a fat banana as fast and as efficiently as he could.

I felt my balls tingle for release, and I started humping up at him. That just got him sucking even faster. It didn't matter that I was coming. I knew I was just starting to get hot and that it was going to be a long night. My dick stiffened even more, and I arched myself up at him, splattering his mouth and throat with a forceful blast. He was so excited that he just kept piston-sucking my rod, even after I fell back on the mattress.

Then Tommy fell alongside me on the bed, licked his lips, and looked up at me with this silly smile. I took hold of his huge fuckpole. Normally I would have been anxious to return the favor and enjoy a taste of that overgrown guy gourd. But there was a different kind of chemistry working that night. Part of it was because Billy was there. Even fast asleep, he kept things extra hot.

I looked over at our sleeping friend. He was still lying on his stomach, and the round, firm cheeks of his ass were propped up invitingly, teasingly. If his buns were going to tease me, somebody's buns were going to pay!

My dick always stays hard for a while after I come. If I'd been straight, girls would've liked me because they sometimes take three-and-a-half years to come. Now, as I looked at those voluptuous Billy-buns across the room, my hard-on hardened even more. I let go of Tommy's cock and grabbed a handful of his left buttcheek, rolling him over onto his stomach.

He was too surprised to react. A quick coating of lube and my prong was poking at the tender opening between his warm meaty cheeks.

"Ohhh," he cried as I squeezed in the head, then slid the hard shaft halfway home. I gave him a full minute to relax, then went in all the way, kneeling above him and crossing my legs over his to pin him down. He groaned softly into the mattress as I started to fuck him.

I fucked the way he had sucked—no fooling around or teasing. I just kept glancing over at Billy's delicious body and driving my dick into Tommy faster and faster.

When I felt my second load coming, I fucked even harder. Tommy grabbed a pillow and buried his face in it as he moaned. He seemed to melt as I hammered away. I felt that magic click that means my cannon is about to fire, and I rose up higher on my arms so I could watch my hard plunger drill his quivering butt. Again and again I drove my load home, draining every drop from my overheated balls.

When I stretched out beside him, I noticed that Tommy's cock was soft and shriveled to Cuban-banana size. I guess Beastie realized that it was going to have to play second fiddle for once.

I went to the bathroom and washed my proud equipment and splashed some water on my face. Instead of being tired, I was now wide awake.

Tommy and I talked and relaxed for a while in bed. Then my all-time-best performance continued. My boyfriend started playing with my cock—not knowing enough to let sleeping dogs lie—and there it went again! It uncoiled and expanded in his groping hand. To be honest, my cock didn't feel sensitive anymore. But it was into more action, and so was I!

The more my prong thickened and stiffened, the more Tommy

scrunched down toward the bottom of the bed. By the time it was standing at full attention, all plump and pink and looking brand-new, Tommy was again bent over between my legs. He looked up at me and said, "I guess I could suck on it a *little* more."

"That's what it's there for," I said. And back he went to work. This time there was no rush. He sucked slowly and lovingly, playing gently with my balls, making it last. When I came, it was a quick, one-shot load. But this time Tommy kept my stiff rod in his mouth while he furiously beat his own meat.

All of a sudden Tommy groaned. Then the hot load he'd been holding back all night splashed against me.

Before we got to sleep there was one last, long, dreamy fuck. I fucked him again on his stomach, but this time slowly, with whispers and kisses. Four orgasms in one night, my personal record.

It was dawn. Except for birds chirping, the only sound was the surf. Tommy was asleep, and I looked at Billy sleeping across the room and pretended that it would always be like that—just the three of us.

Afterword

Life in a Porn Magazine Office
JR

As a college Freshman in the 70s, I passed the same newsstand every day, and one day I was stopped in my tracks. There, alongside the familiar straight porn monthlies, was a glossy magazine with a near-naked man on the cover. It took a few days before I had the nerve to buy it. I know now that it wasn't one of the first gay monthlies that appeared in the 70s, *Mandate, Blueboy*, and *In Touch*. Rather it was one of the hit-and-miss irregularly published magazines that could be traced to box numbers in New York, California, and Florida. They were sketchy but they marked the start of gay print porn.

After college, searching for work, I found an ad in an alternative weekly calling for freelance porn writers. The small company in New York's Greenwich Village turned out straight but kinky pulp paperbacks and I wrote two. They liked my work but I didn't like their long, long delay in making payments.

Fast forward. After I worked many years in boring corporate publishing, the company where I worked moved out of town and I woke up to new possibilities. A literary publisher offered a modest contract to finish editing a book, and then in a gay newspaper, I saw a classified ad seeking an associate editor for porn magazines.

The world of porn opened up to me, leading to a dozen years in the business. The company was Mavety Media and they cranked out more than fifteen straight magazines, including such big sellers as *Juggs, Leg Show,* and *Tight.* I was recruited for the gay magazines, including *Torso, Mandate, Playguy, Honcho, Inches, Black Inches, Latin Inches, Stallion, Uncut,* and *All Man.* Most were put together in the office, but others were created by outside "packagers" who delivered complete contents to our art department.

No film or photography took place in the office. Each magazine showcased a type of model. For example, *Playguy* focused on young pretty twinks, while *Torso* featured handsome gym hunks. Each seven or eight page photo display began with a theme, like a mechanic in a garage in *Honcho,* and ended with hard dick shots. Two local photographers supplied us with new photosets at full price, selected by our art directors. Porn video companies, mostly in California but plenty elsewhere, gave us free photosets of various quality, taken of their porn stars in return for our publicizing their latest films. I've heard directors say that their on-location photos in our magazines led to healthy video sales. One director working mostly in Brazil supplied us with hot Latinos; there were black models straight from the 'hood; smooth, gleaming East European models from Bel Ami; and cut-rate photos of European amateurs from a gay couple, not the most polished but the most authentic.

What mattered most to me and two other associate editors was editing submitted porn stories—this was still snail mail days— and getting them into our magazines. There was a belief in the industry that gay porn fans wanted more written contents than you'd put in straight magazines, and we were using three or four stories per issue. We didn't pay much but the magazines in George Mavety's empire did pay...unlike some in the business.

Each week we got stacks of mail. Aside from love and marriage proposals for the models, much of what we received were stories, and you can imagine the variety. At the far end of the range were terrible efforts, mangled prose and no sex or, worse, bad sex. There was one person whose writing was so bad that almost every sentence needed a fix, and yet his ideas for setting, circumstance and sexual tension were so good that I could turn his work into hot porn. The bulk of submissions were in the middle range, needing corrections, tightening, sometimes a key sentence or two. There were a few contributors who were women and whose writing was pretty good, sometimes good enough to print. What women, whatever their sexuality, lacked was a description of the cock, and of the progress and explosion of the orgasm. Overall, nice writing but skipping the messy male stuff. At the golden, blissful end of the contributor's mail was the rare, beautifully written, red-hot story, with nothing to edit except typos. There were also stories that were well-written but not erotic at all. We editors didn't have time to write a whole sex scene or two. But it costs nothing to send a talented writer praise and encouragement for their writing—and most of the time they are quite young.

Once I gave a talented young writer high praise for his writing. Months later I received a letter from his sister thanking me for that letter because he was young and in his last days, and the kind words meant everything to him. The worst years of AIDS affected everyone. In the office, we lost two editors and two artists. For years we had subscribers adding condoms to their stories—it only takes a sentence.

Magazine editors hate the word "formula" but here are the basics of a porn story. There should be a clear setting, circumstances and characters early on. A minor sex or near-sex scene on page two or three hooks the reader and promises him more. The big payoff is obvious and should be described in detail. That's the framework. The heart of the story is the spark of one's memory or imagination.

Our magazines also took a smaller number of "socially redeeming" articles and reviews, with writing as good as you'll find anywhere, including book reviews by Charles Jurist, Ian Young, and Kevin Bentley.

George Mavety, the Canadian turned American entrepreneur, ran his porn empire like a tight ship, right down to the old-fashioned punch-card clock recording employees' hours. He reportedly had multiple houses and wives in different countries. Legend has it that he brought the first issue of *Mandate* around to newsstands himself, taking a bet on the emerging gay market. His 300-pound bulk was impressive in his expensive suits, and so was his high-end cologne. He had a defrocked priest friend who dressed in black and red monsignor's robes. If he wanted to see you, he would call for you on a loudspeaker, and like Mussolini he had a long, long hallway which you had to travel before reaching his oversized corner office. But he had his imperial charm. Before I left the company, I gave him the honest compliment that there was no prejudice of any kind in his business, and he answered "And there never will be." Once he saw the four gay editors meeting in a conference room and said in his theatric pompous voice, "I have no complaints about the gay magazines, except: Where was I when they were handing out those large penises." The small locked refrigerator in his office was a mystery until someone discovered it was filled with boxes of candy bars, and he would eat four or five at a time.

At Mavety Media, gays and straights mixed well because almost all liked the sex-charged, subculture atmosphere. There was a young straight blond named Eric who I found very hot but I couldn't seduce. Luckily, he agreed to be a model for kinky *Leg Show* magazine. In the (off premises) photoshoot, three naked girls stripped Eric and dressed him in lacey panties and knit leotards—with his family-size hardon sticking up. There was another attractive young straight, a British freelance writer, who stopped by my desk one day and asked if he could submit gay stories. I said "Sure," but asked if he could write gay porn. His perfect answer was, "It's all about dick."

Editing story submissions and proofing two rounds of our magazines really was a full-time job, but on our own time we could write and submit stories and articles for extra cash. I had stories—including most in this book—and nonfiction in some of our magazines and in *Blueboy* under the name "JR" or "Junior Williams."

Proofing was something we took very seriously but one time we failed big-time. It wasn't a writing error we missed, but a front cover photo. The smooth beautiful model was holding a towel in front of him. Cock can never be shown legally on a newsstand magazine. But it wasn't until we got freshly printed copies of that issue did we see it: a small but unmistakable bit of the head of the cock was peeking around the edge of the towel. My first thought was that, if we were fired, at least unemployment insurance wasn't much less than our starvation wages. For days and weeks we waited to be summoned by George's loudspeaker. But it was missed by everyone—and on newsstands across the country our cover boy flashed America.

128

There was a powerful and hot woman editor who was the genius behind some high circulation straight magazines. She was a celebrity and turned heads on the street, and for protection carried a little Derringer pistol. Once a lusty young biker pleasured her in her office while I guarded the locked door for half an hour.

Models occasionally visited the office. Once a famous young guy and girl porn couple from Italy stopped by, looking for film work. Our straight editors could only refer them to film companies. But before they left word got out and employees found excuses to gather outside their offices and cubicles, all down the long hallway. It was like a homage to porn royalty.

One time a woman who posed for *Juggs*, the enormously endowed "Leatha Weapons," was waiting for an editor and she noticed me staring at her gigantic tits. She said, "You want to see them, don't you?" I said yes, she took them out, and I had my hands around what felt like two basketballs. My straight friends love that story.

One of our editors met a legal-aged, rosy-cheeked, all-American boy who was interested in being a model. When he showed up in the office, an art director immediately put him in touch with one of our photographers. He wound up being a cover boy for one of our magazines, and then for the popular women's magazine *Playgirl*.

The photographers had their own stories about models. One guy told us that he met a good-looking kid from rural upstate New York at a bar and the young man made an appointment for a photo session. He showed up at the studio with two friends but decided he couldn't go through with it. But one of his friends, a knockout beauty, posed for the first of several photosets and twice was a *Playguy* cover boy.

Once I covered a porn shoot for an article in *Torso*. The director made sure we all knew everyone in the East Village loft. In fact, the star of the scene, Gus Mattox, came over and made small talk with me. A popular muscle hunk at forty, Mattox's real name was kept top secret because he was also an actor on Broadway. His young partner in the scene looked smooth, but up close you could see his entire body was shaved. The film crew put myself and an *Adult Video News* reporter in a corner where the camera would not go. Finally, they called "Action." To me, the bright lights, the choreographed moves, the stop-and-starts, and the director's instructions were all as sexy as open-heart surgery. But the stars performed perfectly. When it was over, I was surprised that Gus Mattox came over to me again for small talk, but this time he was naked and sweaty. What a pro!

This book of stories was first published when I learned about Masquerade Books, a 1990s mass market publisher of mostly porn paperback originals. Aside from dozens of straight and straight S&M titles (always more S&M than you'd think), there were a few dozen lesbian porn books under the Rosebud imprint. There was a similar amount of non-porn gay fiction and nonfiction under the imprints Hard Candy and Richard Kasak Books, including works by Felice Picano, Samuel R. Delany, Robert Patrick and Pat Califia. But it was the Badboy imprint that produced over a hundred titles, including original books by John Preston, Max Exander, Lars Eighner, and Clay Caldwell. Masquerade paid on publication, which attracted writers, and should be remembered for their contribution to gay history. The late Max Exander was my longtime friend, and I know he would want me to out him at this time. He was the prolific San Francisco writer Paul

Reed who wrote the first novel about AIDS, *Facing It*, for Gay Sunshine Press. I myself used a pseudonym because this book was coming out at the exact same time as a long-awaited literary book I edited. However, I always put my real name in the masthead of many Mavety magazines over the years, which easily means over a million times.

Unfortunately, Masquerade Books are surprisingly hard to find and often expensive when you do locate them. No doubt it is because of their fragile pulp paperback format. That's why this Rebel Satori reprint and its quality production is so welcome.

Over time the Internet was taking a toll on newsstand sales and a number of our magazines were dropped, and employees were laid off. I wound up freelancing for our remaining magazines, which used more photosets from the still successful Bel Ami. Then I met Ms. Powerbosom.

The straight magazines *Big Butt* and *Big Black Butt* were packaged by the large and earthy Ms. Powerbosom. She found plenty of large-butted women for her kinky monthlies, and was a model and writer herself. But she desperately needed a proofreader. For about a year she emailed me issues the evening before her deadlines and I'd spend an all-nighter fixing her hilarious big butt stories.

Maybe it's a good thing that George Mavety never saw the final demise of his company. At 300 pounds he should have known better than to play tennis on a ninety-degree day.

I heard from someone who knows that those last issues of *Torso*, *Mandate*, and *Playguy*, put together by three longtime porn editors, were actually successful. In other words, even in the age of Internet and streaming, there is a market for a few gay magazines featuring hot stories and photos, articles and reviews if only a publisher would take up the challenge. For now, our magazines were made to last and you can find copies, many in mint condition. Look first at the website *gaybackissues.com*. It is ironic that the best way to find our magazines is by the Internet.

The Library of Homosexual Congress, an imprint of Rebel
Satori Press, preserves and promotes classic and provocative
works of gay literature and nonfiction, with focuses on the
AIDS crisis, the nascent gay rights movement as well as
irreverent works of sexual culture and groundbreaking titles
that deserve renewed attention.

Curated by Tom Cardamone and Sven Davisson